THE

HERETICS

HYMNAL

Also by Ken Dalton

Fiction

<u>Pinky and Bear Mystery Series</u>

The Bloody Birthright

The Big Show Stopper

Death is a Cabernet

The Tartan Shroud

Brother, can you spare a dime?

The Unsavory Critic

<u>Casper Potts Series</u>

Casper Potts and the Ladies' Casserole Club

Non-Fiction

Polio and Me

THE

HERETICS

HYMNAL

Ken Dalton

Different
Drummer
Press

ISBN 978-0-578-96836-0
• Humorous—Mystery—Fiction. 2. Pinky—Delmont (Fictional character)—Fiction. 3. Bear—Zabarte (Fictional character)—Fiction. 4. Flo Sonderlund (Fictional character)—Fiction. 5. Carson City, Nevada—Fiction. 6. Nuremberg, Germany—Fiction. 7. Zeppelin Field—Fiction. 8. Congress Hall—Fiction. I. Title.

ACKNOWLEDGEMENTS

This novel came together with the help and assistance from the good people of Wittenberg and Nuremberg, Germany.

To Wittenberg where the church still stands where Martin Luther posted his 95 theses on the church door. Also, the spot where he burned The Pope's notification to inform Luther that he had been excommunicated. In the 1520's, that meant he was now a heretic and could be killed by anyone at anytime. Luther's life was now in the hands of John the Steadfast, Prince Elector of Saxon, and an advocate of Luther's religious position. Prince John the Steadfast's protection was the single reason that Martin Luther died of natural causes at age 74.

To Nuremberg where after WW II, the city fathers decided to retain Congress Hall and Zeppelin Field to remind all future visitors to Nuremberg of Hitler's insanity.

To my artistic son who creates the provocative covers that turn each of my publications into works of art.

To the unsung members of the editing staff for another exceptional picky job to prepare this book for publication.

Finally to Dr. Ye, and the staff, nurses and pharmacists, for my many cancer-free years since my remission.

This book is dedicated to Sarah Brown, my dear friend who wrote her Em Hansen series under the non de plume of Sarah Andrews.

All of the words in my books were written by me, but it took a village of writers, meeting every two weeks, to keep my works careening toward completion. Sarah was my toughest, and most respected critic, and her suggestions were always spot-on.

As I write these words, some two years after the airplane crash that killed Sarah and her family, I am still recovering from the heartbreaking loss of a respected writer, an esteemed critic, and a true friend.

CHAPTER ONE

Flo Sonderlund—Carson City, Nevada

Bear usually writes these pages but Helmut's phone call came in while my man was out buying a set of new tires for his beloved truck and I was the one who first heard Helmut's tale.

Actually, the moment Bear left our place, I was looking forward to a few hours of quiet vacuuming before the endless noise of the Red Sox baseball game took over my world. Don't get me wrong, I like a good game of baseball, just not baseball, baseball, baseball, hour after hour.

But before I get into Helmut's call, I know that there are many out there, like my hairdresser, who think it is unusual that a woman with a PhD in Philosophy could find happiness living with a man who goes by the name of Bear. Also, that I happily spend much of my free time pushing a vacuum around the living room and picking Bear's dirty socks off the bedroom carpet.

In fact, that was almost the exact question posed to me by Tory, the woman who for the past six years has been doing my wash and set every Wednesday at the Silver Dollar Beauty Salon.

To provide Tory a truthful answer, I had to go back a few years, all the way to the days after I received my PhD.

It didn't take me too long to discover that the only gainful employment opportunities available to a PhD in Philosophy were to teach at the University level. And it took me even less time to discover that those positions, especially for a woman, were few and far between.

After six months of no income, and a staggering amount of student debt, I put a frame over a copy of my degree and hung it on the wall adjacent to the large griddle where I flipped hamburgers at a local fast-food joint.

All the second half-year of earning my living cooking burgers brought me was waves of depression. I had days when I didn't want to get out of bed in the morning. Finally, I went to a doctor, who sent me to a shrink, who diagnosed I had cyclothymia, a rare type of cyclical depression. Those who have cyclothymia exhibit some of the same traits as bipolar disorder, but the high-low swings are not as wide as those with full blown bipolar disorder.

As I honestly considered my shrink's diagnosis, I could see that as a child I had experienced mood swings, but I thought they were just part of being a teenage girl.

How did I handle my diagnosis of cyclothymia? At the beginning, not very well. To escape my future as a fast-food queen, I rushed into a marriage, that as I look back, even the minister could see was sure to fail. Then, six months after my divorce, I married again and all I got from that disaster was the need to consume endless bottles of red wine to get through the day.

After my second divorce, I moved to Los Angeles where finally something positive happened that changed my life. I was living alone. Next door to my latest boyfriend. He and I were on the brink of sliding down another slippery slope, when Bear Zabarte came into my life. My knight in shining armor, and rescued me from my cycle of depression.

That's the short version of my life, but I'll bet you have a few questions concerning my relationship with Bear.

First off: is his name really Bear? That's an easy one. His parents, immigrants from the Basque region of Spain, named him Benate and that translates to Bear in English.

Next: yes, I have always been aware that Bear's IQ is not stellar.

Finally: yes, I understand that Bear's language is crude and he uses improper syntax.

However, there are some fabulous upsides to my man. He's extraordinarily street smart, the kind of intellect one needs to survive in the murky world that surrounds his boss, Pinky Delmont, an ethically challenged lawyer.

And, as an extra added attraction, in addition to Bear's physical strength, my man is drop-dead handsome.

But most importantly, Bear finally offered me some stability, a refuge that I had unconsciously been searching for since childhood.

So here I am, living in Carson City, Nevada, with Bear, a man who adores me doesn't give a damn that I have a PhD in Philosophy.

But enough of that.

I was lost in thought pushing the vacuum through the living room when the phone rang. A touch annoyed at the uninvited intrusion into my personal time, I turned off the vacuum, grabbed the phone and snapped, "Hello."

"Flo?"

"Yes."

"Is Bear there?"

I was pretty sure I recognized Helmut Kaufmann's voice, but it pissed me off that he didn't say hello Flo, or how are you doing? No, whatever Helmut had to get off his chest was so important and Bear was the only person in the world that could help him. Well, two could play that game.

I curtly asked, "Who is this?"

"Helmut. Flo you know me. Helmut Kaufmann."

"Are you the same Helmut Kaufmann that we got off a murder one charge a couple of years ago?"

"Flo, I need to talk to Bear, like right now."

"Sorry. Bear's out. Bye now."

He cried, "Flo, please don't hang up."

The tone of his voice sounded so close to total panic that I softened my tone. "Okay, Helmut, what's bugging you."

"Flo, I think I've done something really stupid again, and since Bear helped me out the last time, I figured he'd know what I should do this time."

I considered reminding Helmut that Bear and I work as equal partners on our investigations, but Helmut was a male and males were known to be both chauvinistic and stubborn when talking to females. "Helmut, he won't be back for an hour. You're stuck with me or you'll have to call back later."

"I can't do that, Flo, I need advice now."

"Okay, fire away."

Helmut paused, and then said, "As you recall, a few years ago I went to my brother's

5

home, walked into his office and when I saw he'd been shot, I rushed to his side."

"Yes, I remember. You walked through a pool of your brother's blood, picked up the murder weapon, and then called Bear."

"Right, but that was then."

Oh-oh, here comes the other shoe. "Helmut, as you said, that was years ago."

"Flo, I fear I'm facing a similar dilemma."

"Helmut, don't tell me you're standing in a pool of blood next to a second brother's lifeless body."

"No. This time it's my uncle. And he wasn't shot. He was strangled."

"I'm sure Bear would tell you to jump in your car and immediately drive to Pinky's office."

"But I can't do that."

"Why."

"Because I'm calling you from Nuremberg, Germany."

"Let me be sure I understand what you just said. You're calling me from Nuremberg, Germany, and you're standing next to your dead uncle who's been strangled?"

"Correct."

"And what did Bear tell you a few years ago when you called him?"

"First I followed Bear's instructions concerning my shoes and the murder weapon.

Then he told me to get my ass out of my brother's house as fast as I could."

I hesitated for a moment to think, and Helmut panicked. "Flo, are you still there?"

"Calm down. Exactly where are you in Nuremberg?"

"Inside my uncle's used bookshop."

"And you are alone?"

"Yes, except for my deceased uncle, I'm alone."

"Okay. Assuming you didn't touch the body, the first thing you—"

"Flo, I did touch the body."

"Why did you touch your uncle?"

"I wasn't sure he was dead so I removed the wire from his neck and tried mouth-to-mouth resuscitation. Sadly I was too late."

Mouth-to-mouth resuscitation? I tamped down a growing tone of concern in my response. "Helmut, what the police look for in a murder are opportunity, means, and motive. As far as they're concerned, you're in Nuremberg inside your uncle's shop so that takes care of the opportunity. Next, you had the means, the wire you removed from his neck. And you left your DNA on the body. All that's left for them is to come up with a plausible motive and you'll spend the rest of your days inside a German prison."

"Flo, don't chastise me, just tell me what to do next."

"Do what Bear told you the last time you called him. Get your ass out of Germany as fast as you can and the minute you arrive in Carson City, head to Pinky's office."

CHAPTER TWO

Pinky Delmont—Carson City, Nevada

Following two glorious weeks in San Francisco, the home of epicurean delights paired with outstanding wines, first-rate theater, and a world-class symphonic orchestra, my cynical outlook had turned almost optimistic when I reached my law office located in Carson City, the mundane seat of government for the State of Nevada.

While Carson City was mundane, the town was perhaps less tedious than Montpelier, Vermont, the smallest state capital of these United States of America.

I eased my brand-new Mercedes EQS into my personal parking slot, the newest car on my growing roll of impressive vehicles. This vehicle, the first EQS580 4Matic shipped west of the Mississippi, produces 516 horsepower, and is far and away a more exclusive car than my old Tesla Model S.

Even in Carson City, where I had owned the first Tesla Model S, the backward capitol had so many Teslas that they were nearly as prolific as the Toyota Prius.

So that very morning, as I crossed the city limits where I practiced law, my new $124,000 vehicle turned the heads of many a pedestrian, which was, of course, the sole reason why I purchase all my motor vehicles.

With a newfound bounce in my step, I walked into my office building through the entrance and was delighted to see that my office majordomo, Lu Yong was sitting at her desk with her usual air of strong self-control. Without question, Lu is the most efficient legal secretary in the State of Nevada, but it is a pity that she almost never smiled.

In fact if you looked up the word stoicism in Webster's Dictionary, you would likely find a picture of Lu Yong, the Asian beauty who effectively guarded my gate during my absence.

Euphorically, I greeted her with a smile. "Lu, how are you on this beautiful morning?"

I hoped she would respond to my query with a happy expression, but she only provided her standard perfunctory nod to acknowledge my greeting.

I continued, "Lu, I will spend my morning working on the closing argument for the O'Leary case and do not wish to be disturbed."

Again, Lu nodded without uttering a word.

I unlocked my office door and entered my sanctuary. One might ask why I lock the door to my office. The simple truth is I lack confidence in the local crew that cleans my complex three times a week. Fourteen months ago, I was positive that I detected a minuscule drop in the contents of my favorite bottle of single malt Scotch. From that day on, each time I leave my office for more than three days, I secure my personal office door, just in case my suspicions are correct.

For the first time in a fortnight, I sat down behind my beautiful, over-sized, hand-rubbed, mahogany desk and leaned back recalling my much-needed vacation. Following a moment of reflection, I picked up my phone and placed a call to my favorite ex-wife's private number.

"Hello?"

"Ah Willow, the love of my life, I called to wish you a good morning. Just hearing the melodious sound of your voice has washed away all the feelings of loss I felt during our two-week separation."

"Pinky, I'm right in the middle of a meeting with my staff and unlike you, I don't have time to wander around San Francisco for two weeks."

"My love, I fully understand that you are driven by your professional responsibilities as the District Attorney of our county. The reason for my call is to ask if you will be free later today for lunch. I seek some personal time together so we can discuss an improvement concerning our relationship. Tell me you'll rendezvous with me for lunch today."

Willow responded, "I will call you about about lunch later. Goodbye"

"In fact, my love, I plan to drive to Reno so we can revisit that little French Bistro you love."

Her mellifluous tone turned to a harsh whisper, "Pinky, I told you I'll call you back after my meeting."

I heard a click and she was gone. I sat back, savoring the mental image that the beautiful Willow would soon be at my side. My rumination as to why I had ever agreed to a divorce was interrupted by a light knock at my door, followed by Lu's voice, "May I enter?"

My door opened and without looking up, I snapped, "Lu, I thought you understood that I was not to be disturbed."

"I apologize, but if you recall, many months back you gave me legal advice concerning the rights of the father of my child."

"I recall," responding as tentatively as I could. Seven months ago I had spent nearly an hour of my valuable time on Lu's delicate legal question, pro bono I might add. "Has something new happened that changes the situation concerning your child's father?"

For the first time in my memory, Lu's eyes sparkled with life. "Yes! Last night he phoned and asked me to marry him."

A touch startled, I said, "Are you telling me that he proposed over the phone?"

"He did! His airplane arrives from Boston today and I need to know if—"

The ringing of my office phone interrupted Lu in mid-sentence. The phone rang a second time, then a third. Lu did not make a move to pick up the phone. By the fourth ring, I decided we had reached an impasse to see which one of us blinked first.

With an air of disdain, I lifted the receiver and waved Lu out of my inner sanctum.

"J. Pincus Delmont here. How may I help you?"

"Herr Delmont, my name is Joseph Bauman. I am the, how would you say in your country, the lead detective assigned to the Kriminalpolizei section of the Bavarian State Police in Germany. It's an investigative organization you may know as the Kripos."

The Bavarian State Police? "Should I address you as Lead Detective Bauman, or Herr Bauman?"

"Just Detective Bauman."

His tone made his response a near demand. I sat back and summoned up a metal image of the man on the other end of this conversation. From the slight quaver in his voice, I pictured Detective Bauman as an older man, in his late fifties to sixties, extremely formal, and very, very German.

"Detective Bauman, as we have never met, nor have I visited your country, the investigative organization you called the Kripos is not familiar to me. But that aside, what can I do for you?"

"I am in charge of the investigation concerning the strangulation of a used bookstore owner in Nuremberg."

"Pardon me, Detective Bauman, I thought you said that you were with the State Police of Bavaria. Why are you investigating a murder in the city of Nuremberg?"

"Ah, I see an explanation is in order. In Germany, the larger cities have a local police force to take care of traffic accidents and other minor offenses. The state police force, however, is responsible for all major crimes such as murder."

At that point, I was struggling to figure out how he got my telephone number, or more importantly, why had he called me? "Excuse me, Detective Bauman, Have I missed something? I am an attorney in Carson City, Nevada. Why have you called me?"

"You say you have never visited Germany?"

"No, I have never had the pleasure of traveling to your country. Why do you ask?"

"Herr Delmont, I seek a reason as to why your name and phone number would be in the Contacts section of an iPhone we discovered at the site of a murder."

My name and number in an iPhone?

Totally mystified, I responded, "Detective, I have no idea."

"As I stated previously, I am investigating the murder of the owner of a used bookshop. Does the name—"

I shouted, "Stop right there. At this point in our conversation, and as I have given you my name as required by law, I decline to answer any more of your questions."

Total silence followed, as if this German detective was not used to anyone refusing to answer his questions.

"Herr Delmont, you do not understand. As a lead detective with the Bavarian State Police I have absolute authority. You must answer all questions I ask of you!"

"Detective Bauman, perhaps you do not understand. In my country if a police officer asks a citizen a question, and once that citizen has giving the officer his or her name, the aforementioned is not required to answer any questions. As I am a citizen of the United States, I refuse to answer."

"But…but I…Herr Delmont, I apologize. We have similar rights in Germany, but those rights concerning silence are for suspects. I am sorry for my ignorance concerning your legal rights."

"Excellent! Now that we have agreed there are differences between the United States and Germany, I accept your apology. Moving on, Detective, as we are both an integral part of our legal systems, go ahead and ask me your question again."

There was a pause, as if the German detective was trying to decide if I was playing with him. "I thank you for your cooperation. Herr Delmont, are you familiar with a man named Konrad Kaufmann?"

A curious chill worked down my spine. Kaufmann? A few years ago, I represented a client named Helmut Kaufmann who I had extracted from a trumped-up murder charge. Could it be possible that the Nuremberg murder victim and Helmut were related?

"Detective, I can inform you that I have never known, nor met, nor communicated in anyway with a man named Konrad Kaufmann. Is he an integral part of your investigation?"

"Konrad Kaufmann was the murder victim!"

I said, "This has all been very interesting, but as I stated, I do not know the man and I am a few minutes away from an important meeting with a client.

"Herr Delmont, before you go I do have a few more question that I hope you will be kind enough to answer. My concern is not only the murder of Konrad Kaufmann, but das motiv einer tat."

"Detective, as I am not up to speed with your native tongue, would you please translate that for me?"

"I apologize. Das motiv einer tat means the motive for the deed."

"I see. So you are talking about the motivation for the murder that you are investigating. What have you discovered so far?"

"Herr Delmont, do you play poker?"

After decades of dealing with law enforcement, I was well aware that the best detectives will attempt to confuse the people they are interviewing by posing unexpected questions. Detective Baumann's query was a classic example of that gambit, so I continued cautiously. "As gambling is legal in the State of Nevada, I do occasionally sit in on a game of Texas Hold'em. Why do you ask?"

"I wanted to be sure you would understand the following poker idiom, 'I am going to lay my cards on the table.'"

"Detective, I am very familiar with that expression. Please continue."

"My investigation has led me to believe that the murder victim possessed a book by Martin Luther that is considered extremely valuable."

"Just how valuable?"

The detective paused. "If the book could be authenticated, perhaps many, many millions of Euros. I am positive that the book is the motiv einer tat!"

My interest perked up. "So you feel the shop owner was murdered for the Martin Luther book?"

"You are correct. However, Herr Delmont, I have not been totally honest with you."

By this point in our conversation I felt we were finally getting to the reason the man had called me. "There's more?"

"Herr Delmont, we have discovered some evidence that leads us to believe that the murder of Konrad Kaufmann was committed by—"

My intercom buzzed.

"Excuse me, Detective, but I have to pause for a moment. Please hold."

I pushed the intercom button and barked, "Lu, you better have a good reason to buzz me as you know that I am presently engaged on a phone call."

"Pinky, stop using that nasty tone when talking to me. The reason I interrupted is that Willow is on line two."

"Tell her I am busy and I will call her back."

"But she told me that you asked her to call you as soon as possible."

I snapped, "I am very aware of what I told Willow. As I said, I am in the middle of an important phone call. Do not disturb me again under any circumstances."

I hit the line one button and said, "Detective, I am back. Please finish your sentence."

"We have evidence that leads us to believe that the murder of Konrad Kaufmann was committed by his nephew, Helmut Kaufmann, a man who lives in Carson City, Nevada."

Finally, I understood the reason for the German Detective's phone call. "You said, Helmut Kaufmann lives in Carson City and my office is in Carson City! That is an amazing coincidence. Detective Bauman, please go back to the moment before we were interrupted. Are you at liberty to tell me more information as to why you are so sure that the Martin Luther book was the motive for Konrad Kaufmann's murder?"

"Of course. The murder victim was rumored to have in his possession a valuable first edition, but I need to warn you that according to learned people familiar with such things, finding a first edition of this book after five hundred years would be the equivalent of spotting a dinosaur grazing on the flora in a Nuremberg Stadtpark."

I smiled as I pictured a giant brontosaurus nibbling the shrubbery that lines my driveway.

"Herr Delmont, as I was saying . . . please excuse me for a moment."

I heard him muffle the transmitter and some indecipherable German mumbling, and then he said, "Excuse me, Herr Delmont, an urgent matter has come up that requires my immediate attention so I will have to conclude our call. However, I have a few more items to discuss, so I will call you back as soon as I am able."

CHAPTER THREE

Pinky Delmont—Carson City, Nevada

As I set my phone down, a loud knock at my office door forced the dinosaur image to vanish from my thoughts. The door opened a crack and I heard Lu say, "Please remain there. Mr. Delmont is presently working on a vital closing argument and he may not be available for an unscheduled consultation at this time."

She slipped into my office and shut the door behind her. "You have two choices Pinky: return to my personal problem or would you rather talk with Helmut Kaufmann?"

Her personal problem, or . . . my eyebrows jumped. "Lu, did you say Helmut Kaufmann?"

"I did. I'm sure you remember him, Pinky. A few years ago you defended him when he was accused of murdering his brother."

Between Lu seeking free legal advice, Detective Bauman's enigmatic phone call, and now Helmut Kaufmann, my reservoir of euphoria had all but vanished.

"Lu, please escort Mr. Kaufmann into my office, and I would like you to stay and take notes. As soon as Mr. Kaufmann's concerns have been aired and he has left, I promise I will give you what ever time you need from my busy schedule."

Lu blinked, her only display of emotion, and stormed out of my office.

A moment later, as Helmut Kaufmann crept into my office, I pasted a smile on my face as I greeted my former client. He ignored my offer of a chair and stood with his back to the door, as if he felt better protected by the solid wall of wood. The man seemed almost embarrassed as he stood there clutching a small cardboard box in his hands.

"Helmut, my old friend. As Lu informed you, I am presently working on an important closing argument, however, I always leave a little wiggle room in my busy schedule for a valued client. What sort of situation have you gotten yourself into this time?"

Helmut gulped for air, as if he were a fish just pulled from the water. "I think there might be a warrant out for my arrest."

So hearing the Kaufmann name from two separate sources was not a coincidence. Recalling Detective Bauman's promise that he would soon call me back, I decided to move expeditiously. "A warrant? My good man, what crime are you accused of committing this time?"

"Murder."

Ah ha!

"Helmut, I have just returned from a much-deserved respite from the rigors of my legal practice, so I am not aware that a murder had been committed in Carson City."

"Pinky, not here. The murder took place in Nuremberg, Germany."

The moment he said Nuremberg, Germany, and despite my usually controlled expression, I had to fight to keep the thrill of the hunt out of my response. I leaned forward to take full measure of the man. "And you are concerned that the German police might charge you with that murder?"

"Yes." Then, with a touch of panic in his tone he cried, "Pinky, no matter what the German police say, I DID NOT KILL MY UNCLE!"

While I do not usually tolerate anyone yelling in my office, Helmut was distraught and his unexpected situation could turn into a very large retainer. But first I had to calm my client down. "Helmut, please do not raise your voice again. Remember, I am on your side. Now sit down and tell me everything and be sure to start from the beginning."

He moved to a chair, sat down, and laced his shaking fingers around the box, as if that action might quell the tremors. "Thank you, Pinky."

"You are welcome. Now tell me your story."

"About two months ago, I received a phone call from a man who spoke English, but with a very thick German accent. The man told me that I was his nephew. At that point I was confused, because I never knew I had an uncle. Regardless, the man convinced me that he really was my father's brother because he..."

As Helmut droned on, I sat back and maintained my expression of interest in his story while my mind drifted back to each course I had been served during my dinner at one of the truly outstanding restaurants of the world, Gary Danko's in San Francisco.

"...and then my uncle informed me that he had just been diagnosed with stage four pancreatic cancer and was given but a few months to live so..."

At what finally seemed to be a lull in Helmut's story, I interrupted. "Forgive me, Helmut, but what does all this have to do with a warrant for your arrest?"

"You told me to start at the beginning."

Had I recalled how tedious my previous meetings had been with this client, I would have given him a different instructions, but it was too late now. "You are correct, I did."

But before Helmut continued, Lu cleared her throat. An obvious gesture that I took to mean that she felt her personal needs were more important than listening to a man talk about murdering his long-lost uncle. I flashed her my strongest cease and desist glare, and anticipating my pending call from Willow, I surreptitiously glanced at my watch. Appalled to note that I had less than ninety minutes before our lunch reservation in Reno, I stifled a sigh.

"Helmut, while I still have a few moments to spare for you my time is valuable, so please, cut to the chase."

"I understand. A few days after my uncle's phone call, I received a delivery from FedEx."

He placed the 1x6x8 inch box on my desk and proceeded to open it. "This is what my dying uncle sent me."

I stood, leaned forward, and looked inside the box at what seemed to be the cover of a very, very old book. I started to poke my finger inside, but Helmut cried, "Pinky, DON'T DO THAT! What's inside looks so fragile that I didn't have the courage to pull it out of the FedEx box."

I sat back down and considered my various alternatives. The book Helmut received was more than likely an old, worthless family heirloom from a dying relative. However, the statement made by Detective Bauman about the motive, and how a Martin Luther first edition could be worth multi-millions had piqued my interest.

Manufacturing a disinterested tone, I said, "I am happy you brought the book with you."

As I stared at the FedEx box, I reminded myself that the man sitting opposite me had ended up with a tidy nest egg from his deceased brother's estate, but I also recalled that Helmut had a history of investing poorly. Therefore, my potential client could be with or without the required financial wherewithal that would allow me to mount a proper defense. Some research into the contents of the mysterious box might be worth a few moments of my precious time. I stood up and glanced at my watch. "My goodness! Helmut, I have an important conference call coming up that will involve me in some prolonged legal discussions." I paused for a moment to let him ponder the situation, then I continued, "Lu, I have an idea. Take twenty dollars out of petty cash and treat Mr. Kaufmann to coffee and pastry at that excellent little French bakery down the block."

My phlegmatic majordomo frowned, "Pinky, as we discussed earlier, I have an appointment to meet—"

"Your little break should not take more than fifteen minutes."

Lu glanced at her watch and nodded. "Fine. We'll be back soon."

I not-so-gently pushed them both out of my office. "Now, you two hurry along. There is an incarcerated man who is depending on this conference call to extricate him from his present plight."

The moment my office door closed, I reached into my jacket pocket for my iPhone, turned on the flashlight, and stared inside the FedEx box. There seemed to be a small book that consisted of fewer than ten pages. I could make out some printed words but they looked to be an old German script that was completely indecipherable to me. The contents did seem old enough to have some bona fide value, however, without further research I could not be sure. As I pondered my next move. Suddenly, Florence, popped into my mind, she was a woman who seemed to have been placed on this earth to torment me. However, when I looked beyond her overly developed breasts and her worthless PhD in philosophy, I recalled that she had majored in linguistics with an emphasis in German.

I picked up my phone and dialed her number. After I impatiently listened to many rings, I was about to hang up when she answered.

"Hello."

"Florence, I seek some information."

"Pinky, didn't your mother teach you any manners? What you should have said was, 'Good morning, Florence. How's your day going?' And I would have answered, 'I'll call you back in five minutes when I've finished vacuuming the apartment.' By the way, Pinky, how IS your day going?"

My God, the woman had a way of testing my self-restraint, but at the moment, I needed her. "Florence, sitting on my desk there is a small box. Inside the box is what appears to be a very old book that presents me with more questions than answers. The item looks to be hundreds of years old, consists of less than a dozen pages and on one page I can make out some words but they are German and as you are well aware, French was my language of choice during undergraduate studies, so I am unable to read or translate German."

She said, "Pinky, this is an auspicious occasion. I've found something that you confess is beyond your ability. I hope Bear gets back soon so he can hear this."

"Florence," my anger and voice rose. "Do not cause me to lose my temper."

"Calm down. I was just toying with you. Now, can you read any of the letters to me."

"The cover is so faded I cannot make out a letter, but if I carefully lift the cover with my pen I can see some very faint text in an old

German script. The letters are n-u-n," I lifted the cover higher, "f-r-e-u-t, and the last four are e-u-c-h."

After a moment of silence, a vocal condition that was totally unlike the Florence I knew, she responded, "Nun freut euch is part of a whole sentence, Nun freut euch lieben Christen g'mein. That translated means, Dear Christians, one and all rejoice. Also, Nun Freut Euch, is the title of a hymn written by Martin Luther somewhere during the early 1520's. Can you tell me how many pages make up the book?"

"As all the pages look very fragile I am afraid to take the book out of the box to count them."

Another unexpected pause from Florence, this time even longer than the first. "If you could count the pages and there were ten, I'd get really excited. Where did you get this book?"

"It came to me from Germany via FedEx. Why are the number of pages so important?"

"Because Martin Luther's printed hymnal from the age of the Reformation consisted of eight songs."

I said, "Florence, do you know what the title is in German?"

"The Achtliederbuch, however, it's not possible that you are looking at a real

Achtliederbuch. Pinky, my best guess is that the book you are looking at is a copy. An artificially aged copy. A very good copy. But a copy. A sort of expensive souvenir one would purchase at the Martin Luther museum shop in Wittenberg, Germany."

"Florence, judging by the condition of the pages, what I am staring at does not look like a fake sold in a museum shop."

"Listen to me, Pinky. The original book was printed in Wittenberg, Germany around 1524. It contained eight hymns, four of them written by Martin Luther himself. He published his hymnal to bring religion to the people, in their language, and in a form small enough to carry with them when they attended church. There's no way the book you have in your possession could have survived five hundred years after being stuffed in and out of the pockets of peasant farmers. That said, it should be obvious, to even you that what you are looking at is a copy. Now, if you don't mind, I have to finish cleaning my apartment."

Before I had time to voice my counter argument, the vixen had hung up!

As the man who pays her monthly salary, she should be required by common courtesy, if not the law, to provide me with the information I needed. Evidence to back up her assertion concerning the authenticity of the book in question! Every word out of her mouth seemed to thwart, rather than assist me, the benefactor who paid for the roof over her head. All I wanted was the answer to a single question— did she know of a way to prove this book authentic, or to prove it to be a copy?

Struggling to control my rising anger, but with nowhere else to turn, I punched the keys on my phone that would again connect me with Florence.

CHAPTER FOUR

Pinky Delmont—Carson City, Nevada

Ring!
Ring!
Ring!
Ring!
Ring!
My god, that vixen was avoiding answering the phone because she knew I would call her back.
Ring!
Ring!
Ring!
I was about to throw the phone against the wall and confront Florence in person when she finally answered.

"Hello."

"Florence, due to your irresponsible behavior I am considering replacing you and Bear as my investigative team."

"Pinky, I'm putting the phone on speaker because Bear just walked in the door so he can hear what's going on. Bear, Pinky's going to fire us because I told him I think the book he has is a fake"

I yelled, "Florence, that's not my reason and you know it. I do not understand how you can make your determination without even looking at the book."

"Boss?"

I took a deep breath. "Yes, Bear."

"I don't know what you and Flo are fighting about, but a couple of months ago I decided that I was gonna stop answering the damn phone 'cause every time I picked it up, there was always somebody on the other end, and that somebody was usually you yelling at me and Flo about something stupid."

I cried, "Bear, stop babbling and put Florence back on. I need to talk with her about something important and you have nothing you could possibly add to the conversation."

"Great! You guys go ahead and shoot the bull 'cause that blonde babe on TV with the jiggly boobs just started to sing the National Anthem. When the song's over, the first Red Sox playoff game will start. Don't worry guys, I'll turn the sound down on the TV."

Flo said, "I'm back, but you need to listen to me as to why I think the book is a forgery."

"Go right ahead."

"Pinky, during my undergraduate years, I spent months studying the European Reformation. I'm sure you remember the Reformation, that time around the end of the middle ages when Martin Luther essentially told Pope Leo the tenth to go pound salt?"

"As I am an educated individual, Florence, I have some familiarity with the Reformation."

"I'm happy to hear that, but you may not know the story behind why Luther did what he did. He was ordained as a priest in 1507. However, ten years later, he rejected many of the church's basic precepts. In 1517, in a statement of defiance, he wrote his famous Ninety-five Theses that demanded the Catholic church, and Pope Leo X, make major changes."

Pinky said, "Yes, Florence, I've heard about the Ninety-five Theses that Luther nailed to a church door."

"Great, but I'm just getting to the exciting part. The Pope demanded Luther renounce his writings. He refused. In 1521, Luther appeared before a general assembly of the Holy Roman Empire. After a brief trial, Luther was excommunicated and condemned as an outlaw throughout the Empire. Pinky, the bottom line here is that any citizen of the Holy Roman Empire could kill Luther without legal consequence."

"I will admit that this part of your tale has piqued my curiosity. However, I do not recall hearing that Luther was assassinated."

"That's correct. Frederick the third, Elector of Saxony, the head of state where Luther lived, successfully protected him from all danger and Luther died peacefully at age 62."

"Is class over?"

"Not yet, here's the final punch line to my story. As of today, the Catholic Church has not lifted the 1520 excommunication of Martin Luther."

"Very interesting, but I do not see how your little history lesson proves the book on my desk is a forgery."

"I'm getting there. My Reformation professor, an educator I respect, spent more than thirty years of his life searching up and down Germany for a first edition of the Achtliederbuch. He finally came to the conclusion that it did not exist. Pinky, trust me, if there was a first edition of that book lying around, my professor would have it locked away in his vault."

"So you are telling me that because your old professor could not find an original first edition, there is no possibility that the book I am looking at is the real deal?"

"You've got it, Sparky."

"My good woman, as you are my employee, I demand you show some deference when speaking to me."

"Pinky, get off your high horse. You're no better than the rest of us." Then Bear's booming voice took over. "Babe, I don't want to be a pain in the ass, but you're talking on a cordless phone. How about taking that call down the hall into the bedroom. My game's 'bout to start and between you and the boss I can't concentrate on a damn thing."

Florence cried, "Hold it down, Bear. I only answered the phone because you weren't here."

"But Babe, the big game is starting. Come on. I don't ask for much. Just a couple of times a year, when the Sox get into the playoffs, I want to see 'em on TV and down a couple of brews."

"Bear, you are worthless during the entire baseball season."

"But this is not the regular season. These are the playoffs."

Tired of hearing the bickering between what had to be the most diverse couple on the planet, I yelled, "Florence, as much as I enjoy listening to you two quarrel, I have a law practice to run. I have a final question for you. If the Achtliederbuch were an original, what would its value be?"

After a second or two, she said, "Hard to say off the top of my head, but the word priceless was what my college professor said many times."

"Perhaps I did not make myself clear, Florence. I am seeking a monetary value. For example, if the book were authentic, and I found someone who was eager to purchase it from me, what should my asking price be?"

She snickered, "If you found a person gullible enough to believe the book was authentic, and if you had no scruples, which I know you don't, you could take the sucker for a hundred million, maybe even more."

"Florence, any action on my part to sell the book would not be considered fraudulent as long as I truly believed that the work was authentic."

"Let me know the minute you find someone foolish enough to buy the fake because I have a unicorn horn stored in my closet I'd love to sell them. Now, get off my case so I can finish vacuuming."

CHAPTER FIVE

Pinky Delmont—Carson City, Nevada

On the verge of total exasperation, I concluded my fruitless conversation with Florence. For a moment I stared at the box that might contain something worth in the neighborhood of hundred million dollars, or absolutely nothing, when a light knock on my office door snapped me out of my reverie.

Lu entered followed by Helmut.

She said, "Thank you Pinky, despite my time constraints that was a good idea. Helmut had a tarte tatin and I enjoyed a mille-feuille pastry along with a cup of excellent coffee. Now what?"

Struggling to calm my vexation caused by the two females that I am forced to communicate with more then I care to, I said, "Helmut, sit down. Thank you, Lu, I will call you if I need you."

She started to leave my office, hesitated, then walked up to my desk. "Pinky, earlier you told me that we were going to discuss my situation first. Are you so callous a human being that you can somehow ignore the years of faithful service I have given to you?"

The answer to her question was as obvious as the nose on her face. Helmut was a client who had the money to replenish my depleted coffers while Lu felt that she could use my valuable time to discuss the legal aspects of the pending wedding with the father of her child.

I set my jaw and through tight lips, I hissed, "Lu, once I finish my meeting with Helmut, a man who obviously requires my immediate legal advice, I will provide you with the time you need to discuss your pending event."

"But Pinky, I don't have time to meet with you later. I told you earlier that the father of my child arrives from . . . forget it, I tried!" She turned and stormed out of my office.

Once the door closed, I said, "Helmut, I apologize for my employee's unprofessional behavior. Now, you can continue with the tale of where this old book led you."

"Like I said, whatever was inside that FedEx box looked so fragile I was afraid to pull it out. Then I realized that I might never know what it was if my uncle died before he could tell me. That's when I decided to go to Germany to ask him."

Once I opened the package from my uncle, I decided to go to Germany, to thank him before he succumbed from his pancreatic cancer."

In my opinion, an expensive international flight was a bit over the top when a simple combination get-well, thank you card would suffice. However, from the day I opened my law practice, I had learned that the only thing I could expect from a client was the unexpected. I responded, "So you flew to Germany?"

As Helmut rambled on, I wasn't all that interested in what he had to say until I heard the following: "And then I got down on my hands and knees, put my ear close to his mouth and nose to see if he was breathing."

I jumped up. "Helmut, stop talking and do not utter another word. You need to retain me so any further disclosers on your part will be covered under attorney-client privilege."

"Slow down, Pinky, I don't understand."

"Helmut, the moment you retain me as your attorney, all discussions between us will be confidential. Do you want to retain me as your attorney of record?"

"I think so."

"Then remove a dollar from your wallet and hand it to me."

He did as I requested.

I said, "Thank you. As soon as our discussion has been completed, I will have Lu draw up a standard retainer agreement."

"Will that be necessary?"

"My good man, at the moment I represent you because of the dollar I hold in my hand. However, this dollar only covers you during our initial meeting. To receive my full representation, you will need to sign a retainer agreement. Now, if my memory serves me well, I believe the retainer for your previous murder accusation was in the neighborhood of $150,000. Of course, that was some time ago. Due to the difference in the US and German legal systems, travel and lodging expenses, and other variables to numerous to discuss I fear this time around your retainer will run you $300,000, plus expenses."

Helmut began to breathe rapidly, as if he had just completed running his first marathon. "Pinky, I have enough money in the bank to live on, and a little nest egg invested in Muni bonds, but $300,000 would take everything I have and then some."

"I see. Helmut, at this juncture, I feel it is time to remind you that just a few years ago I successfully defended you against a charge of first-degree murder"

"Pinky, I remember that, but I didn't kill my brother or my uncle for that matter."

"As your attorney, your guilt or innocence is not important to me. I am talking about the time and resources I will have to expend developing an ironclad defense stratagem that will result in your eventual freedom. And do not forget the additional cost that I will incur this time defending you against the German barbarians who have gathered at your gate. Helmut, I do not want to frighten you, but I fear you could be but moments away from incarceration!"

As if Helmut were a puppy whose tail had just been stepped on, an involuntary yelp slipped past his lips.

As moments of silence ticked away, I was about to write out the phone number of the Public Defender, when, with a quivering lower lip, Helmut said, "I guess I could scrape together as much as $250,000, but that would pretty much clean me out."

His offer would more than cover the cost of my new Mercedes, and my vacation in San Francisco. And there was always the chance that the item languishing inside the FedEx box could be worth something.

"Helmut, while you were out I took the liberty of doing a little research on the heirloom your uncle sent you from Germany. I was told that the object is likely of limited value. However, as you are a previous and valued client, I accept your offer of $250,000, and what is inside the FedEx box to make up the difference."

Helmut's face lit up with his gratitude.

I offered my right hand to my newest client to seal the deal. "Helmut, sit down and let us return to Nuremberg. You are in your uncle's bookshop and you find a body on the floor. Once you had determined your uncle was not breathing, did you call the police?"

He shook his head.

"Then tell me what you did next?"

After listening to him recount his movements, I was stunned to learn that my client had placed his fingerprints and DNA all over the dead man, evidence that would tie Helmut to the murder site.

I said, "And then what did you do?"

"I called Bear, but he was out, so I talked to Flo."

That vixen did not mention receiving a call from Helmut. "And what did Florence advise you to do?"

"She told me to get my ass out of Germany as fast as I could, and when I got back to Carson City to see you."

At least she had enough sense to tell Helmut to see me once he returned home. I said, "And you followed her advice?"

"Yes, except after I made my call to Flo, in my panic to get out of there, I accidentally dropped my phone and couldn't find it."

I suppressed an expression of despair. I had agreed to represent a client who claimed he was innocent, but a client who had left enough evidence at the scene of the murder to make my job nearly impossible. More importantly, Helmut could destroy my Carson City record of one hundred percent acquittals concerning capital crimes.

I sighed, "At least you came to me once you arrived home."

"Not exactly. I'm not sure if it was jet lag, or the shock of seeing my uncle's dead body with that wire wrapped around his neck, or the flight to Paris, then on to Reno, but after I arrived in Carson City, I spent a couple of days in bed."

"Helmut, as I am sure you now understand, the German police will likely accuse you of strangling your uncle. They have partial fingerprints, and possibly your DNA. They have your phone. They have your picture and passport number when you entered their country. They . . . hold on, did you pay cash for the cab from the airport to your uncle's bookstore?"

"No. I used my credit card."

"And did you use the same credit card for your return taxi ride back to the airport?"

"I did."

"And the same card for your return flight to the US?"

Helmut's jaw tightened as he realized the evidence trail he had left for the police. "Yes, and I used the same card for my fight to Paris and then to Reno."

I said, "Obviously, the German authorities will be able to track your every move, from your arrival in Nuremberg to your uncle's bookshop and back to Carson City. My good man, in the minds of the German authorities you are the man who murdered your uncle. Frankly, they have everything they need to arrest you except a motive."

"What do you mean by a motive?"

"A reason why you would fly all the way to Germany just to murder your uncle."

"Oh. I see what you mean. But, Pinky, regardless of my lack of motive, this mess sounds very bad for me."

"It is! When did you say you returned to Carson City?"

"A few days ago."

My stomach tightened. The last thing I wanted was to have a client arrested while sitting in my office, a dreadful situation that I was beginning to realize could happen at any moment.

"Helmut, are you familiar with The Old Globe bar?"

"I've never been inside because it always looked me like a dive bar. However, I know where it is located."

"Good. Bear and Flo will meet you at The Old Globe in fifteen minutes." I scribbled an address on a note, placed it inside an envelope and sealed it. "Hand this sealed envelope to Florence, and only Florence, when you meet her at the bar."

Helmut frowned. "I don't understand. What do Bear and Flo have to—"

I said, "Helmut, as we sit here, I am concerned that the German government has submitted an extradition request to our State Department who have likely forwarded the matter to the Department of Justice to begin the extradition proceedings to Germany."

Helmut's jaw dropped. "Extradition? What does that mean?"

"Extradition means if the German authorities have enough evidence that you committed a murder in their country, the United States government will turn you over to them for trial."

He jumped out of his chair and started to wring his hands and pace around my office as if he looked hard enough he might find a concealed escape hatch.

I could see by Helmut's actions that the concept of imprisonment was more than my client could handle. "My good man, by my calculations we could have less than twenty-four hours before a Federal Marshall knocks on your door with a writ from the German government demanding your return to Germany. Now follow my instructions. Go to The Old Globe and wait there for Bear and Flo."

Helmut started to say something but I stopped him. "Helmut, your immediate freedom is at stake. Leave my office at once and walk, no run to The Old Globe."

Finally my admonition sunk in and he sprinted out of my office. The moment my door closed I tried to phone Bear, but his line was busy. While I waited to call again, I went online, looked up extradition, German style, and found:

EXTRADITION TREATY WITH THE FEDERAL REPUBLIC OF GERMANY
This treaty will make a significant contribution to international cooperation in law enforcement. I recommend that the Senate give early and favorable consideration to the treaty and give its advice and consent to ratification.
Signed,
JIMMY CARTER.

Then I scrolled toward the end of the document and found what I was looking for:

Offenses that fall under the June 20, 1978 Extradition Treaty.
   1.Murder.
   2.Manslaughter.

Once I had reviewed the extradition agreement between the USA and Germany, I was positive that I had done the right thing for my client. If he stayed at his home, or remained in my office, he could be arrested and shipped to Nuremberg, Germany, where he would face a charge of first-degree murder!

Finally, I called Bear and he picked up. "Boss, I'm right in the middle of an important meeting."

"Bear, I pay your salary and I am fully aware your important meeting is a baseball game on TV. Now—"

"But boss, the—"

"Shut up and stop calling me boss. You and Florence are to go at once to The Old Globe where you will find Helmut Kaufmann and—"

"Helmut? My old buddy, Helmut Kaufmann? Who'd he kill this time?"

"That woman you live with knows all about Helmut's latest situation."

"Okay, boss."

"Once you are at The Old Globe, Helmut will hand Florence an envelope. She will open the envelope and the three of you will follow the instructions I have written inside. Then—"

"Wow, this is like a treasure hunt. Is it a real treasure hunt, boss?"

Generally, I am not paranoid, but there was an outside chance that the German government might have convinced a Federal judge to tap my phone. The note to Florence was my way of passing on Helmut's destination in a covert way, thus allowing my client to temporarily escape the extradition net and give me the time required to develop a proper defense.

I shouted, "Bear, will you shut up and listen to me! Go to The Old Globe, meet with Helmut and follow the instructions. Once you arrive at the destination, call me on the land line, not your cell phone."

"Why the land line?"

"Because, you dolt, unlike a land line, a cell phone call can be traced to the nearest cell tower. Now hang up and get Helmut out of Carson City."

CHAPTER SIX

Pinky Delmont—Carson City, Nevada

Satisfied I had saved my client from immediate arrest, I spun my chair around, removed a bottle of my favorite single malt Scotch from the credenza and poured myself a modest sip in celebration.

As I finished the amber liquid, my office phone rang. I glanced at my watch. It was too early for Willow. The phone rang again. I waited for Lu to do her job and answer the phone. After the fourth ring, I cursed Lu under my breath and answered the phone. "Law Office of J. Pincus Delmont."

"Ah, Herr Delmont. I am pleased to find you are still in your office at this late hour."

I stood and walked around my desk. "It is nearly noon here in Carson City, Detective." I opened my office door and glanced around the room. Lu was nowhere in sight. "You may have forgotten about the eight-hour time difference between us. That means you are the one who is still in his office at a late hour. What can I do for you?"

"I would like to resume our earlier conversation. I am working on the theory that das motiv einer tat was money and therein lies the irony. Helmut Kaufmann strangled his uncle for his first edition of the Achtliederbuch, but many experts claim, that book does not exist. It seems that Konrad Kaufmann was murdered for no reason."

I sat down and stared at what Detective Bauman considered an obvious forgery in the box resting on my desk.

"Detective, I read somewhere that there was a first edition resting in a museum in Wittenberg."

Bauman chuckled. "Perhaps a second edition, but not a first edition."

"Could you explain to me why that would be impossible?"

"I will try. The Achtliederbuch, the original Martin Luther song book, was published more than five hundred years ago and although many people have searched for years, no one has ever unearthed a first edition. I have to believe Konrad Kaufmann possessed an excellent forgery, one that upon a cursory glance might fool some experts, but a forgery none the less. That point settled, I do have one more item I need to discuss with you. If we are to continue our conversation, what I tell you next must be held in strict confidence. Do you agree? If not, I will hang up and our phone conversation will cease."

Every aspect of my first day back, from Lu's demand for free legal advice, to Helmut's description of his monumental ignorance, and now Detective Bauman's requirement of confidentiality, all seemed designed to strip away the last vestige of my vacation. Anticipating the joy of a rendezvous with Willow, I wanted to avoid further confrontation, but I had to admit that the German detective's challenge had aroused my curiosity.

"Detective Bauman, as an attorney who generally represents clients accused of capital crimes, the majority of my conversations are held in confidence. I agree to your stipulation. Please continue."

For a moment, I listened to the detective's controlled breathing, as if he was pondering just how much he should trust this American attorney. Eventually he said, "My country has initiated extradition proceedings against Helmut Kaufmann. We have overwhelming evidence that he was in his uncle's bookstore around the time he was murdered."

Now assured that my plan to hide Helmut had been the right move for my client, I said, "I can tell you this. Before this call I did meet with a man named Helmut Kaufmann, but as he is now my client, that is all I can tell you."

"Herr Delmont," His voice rose with excitement. "That is precisely why I have called you back."

At this point in our conversation, I felt the need to review the file I had concerning Helmut's previous murder accusation to recall the important details of how I had kept him out of prison. "Detective Bauman, I have a minor office problem that I need to handle. It could take me a couple of minutes. Can you hold?"

"Please go ahead. I will wait."

I hit the hold button, then the intercom. "Lu, bring me the Helmut Kaufmann file." After waiting a few seconds for her response, I stormed out of my office to admonish her and found an empty room. I walked toward the restroom door, knocked, and called, "Lu, are you in the ladies room?"

Dead silence permeated my office. I turned and realized that the top of Lu's desk had been stripped clean of all her personal items. My stomach tightened as I realized that as she had threatened, Lu might have left my office for good. Once again, my legal ship lacked a trusted first mate, a second in command who would maintain the course of my law practice through stormy seas while I was engaged elsewhere.

I sat down at Lu's desk and found the phone number for Rapid Replacement, the catalyst I required to start the grist mill grinding for a successor.

At the end of the second ring, I heard, "Rapid Replacement, Louis Loomer here. When you need a part-time or full-time employee, Rapid Replacement is your solution. How may I assist you to find the perfect employee for your immediate need?"

"Loomer, Pinky Delmont here. I have an important phone call from Germany on hold so I will be brief. I have two immediate needs. First, and this is critical, I require someone to answer my office phone lines. Second, I require a—"

"Pinky? What happened to Lu? Is she ill?"

"Loomer, in case this fact has slipped your mind, the name of your business is Rapid Replacement. I assume that the title means you meet a customer's needs rapidly and do not waste their valuable time by asking inane questions."

Loomer said, "Right. I'll will immediately send you Holly to your location. She will arrive in minutes, however, as she is my personal assistant she will only cover your office needs for today. I cannot afford to lose someone as valuable to my business as Holly indefinitely. I will also begin a search to find you a full-time replacement for Lu. But, and this is a big but, you have a reputation as a difficult employer throughout the environs of Northern Nevada, so my search for an available replacement will need to cover a much larger area, all of Nevada and perhaps even California if needed."

I considered challenging his assessment of me as a difficult employer, but at that point, with Detective Bauman waiting on hold, I didn't have time to argue with him. "Loomer, do what you must, but be sure you understand my requirements. I seek an employee who is capable of navigating my legal ship through a force five hurricane. Do you understand?"

"I understand, but before I begin the search, you need to agree that the cost of my services will be dependent on the size of the territory I need to cover to find your so-called navigator."

"You have already explained that to me!"

"And that you agree to pay the extra expenses I may incur during the expanded search?"

The little people of this world concentrate so hard on tracking their pennies that they forget to watch their dollars. "Loomer, you are testing my patience."

"Pinky, do you agree?"

"I agree."

He responded, "One final item. Once I find you a replacement for Lu, I think you should consider placing that person under a Rapid

Replacement contract. In essence, your legal secretary will work for me, Rapid Replacement, not you. I will pay them. All you have to do is reimburse my company for their salary and benefits."

My office phone rang on line two. Then again. Then a third time.

Loomer said, "Do you need to put me on hold so you can answer that call?"

"Not now." I snapped. ,"I need to complete our discussion first. Now, explain my downside to your proposal?"

I was about to push the flashing button, put the caller on hold, and then listen to Loomer's explanation when the light stopped flashing and the ringing ceased.

Loomer said, "Your cost per employee will increase by fifteen percent."

"The upside?"

"Pinky, you will be relieved of all the day to day concerns for your employee such as, but not limited to, vacations."

Based on the past few years, a fifteen percent increase in cost was minuscule compared to the time I spent fighting over vacation scheduling and the like. But what if Loomer's selection was incompatible with me? There had been moments, not often mind you, but there had been a few times when my employees proved to be incompatible. "Loomer, what if I decide that Lu's replacement and I are not well suited?"

"All you have to do is call me before you tell her, or him, to leave your office. I will send over a temporary replacement and then, within a few days, find you a new majordomo."

At that moment, I felt as if I had discovered the path to employer nirvana. No more concerns about sick days off, vacations, the quality of work—those items would be Loomer's headache. Under his proposed system, I would have the right person guarding my gate no matter what happened. "Loomer, I agree to your contractual plan. Now go out and find me the next Lu Yong."

Returning to my office, I poured a second glass, this time two fingers of my single malt elixir, took a couple of sips and hit the button for line one. "Detective Bauman, I am back. If I recall, you last told me that you have physical evidence that proves my client, Helmut Kaufmann, was in his uncle's bookstore the day he was murdered."

"That is correct."

I was curious where the good detective was going with this theory.

"Detective Bauman, I can tell you this much. Prior to retaining me as his attorney, Mr. Kaufmann and I had a pleasant discussion, but the word Achtliederbuch never came up."

"Herr Delmont, as you informed me earlier that you are the sort of attorney who defends people accused of major crimes, I find it difficult to believe that you and your client would spend your valuable time talking and never once discuss the murder I am investigating."

"Detective Bauman, I said that Helmut Kaufmann and I had a pleasant conversation prior to retaining me as his attorney. Any discussion that we had after he retained me is protected by attorney-client privilege. Now, if you will excuse me, I have to prepare for an important meeting with a client."

"Before you go, I want to thank you for your informative explanation concerning attorney-client privilege. As I stated before, the citizens of the sovereign nation of Germany are members of the European Union, and as such, they do not have the same rights as you do in your country. Please, one last question. Does your attorney-client privilege allow you to tell me where your client is presently located?"

"I am afraid not. And as you have posed a final question, I also have one for you. Why are you so sure that the Achtliederbuch was in the possession of the murder victim?"

"I am sorry, but that information, similar to your attorney-client discussion, is not available. I can tell you this, the force working under me have checked most of the books in Kaufmann's shop and to the best of our knowledge, Luther's Achtliederbuch was not there."

"Excuse me, Detective Bauman, but you have just raised a question. Earlier you claimed you did not feel it was possible that a first edition of the Achtliederbuch existed. Now you just informed me that you had your men search the entire bookstore for the Achtliederbuch. Why would your people spend their valuable time searching for a non-existent book?"

There was a long pause and the detective's lack of response informed me that the old book sitting on my desk just might be the real item, an object worth hundreds of millions of dollars.

Then Detective Baumann said, "At this time I am not at liberty to divulge that information. Herr Delmont, do you have any idea how your name and phone number ended up in an iPhone we discovered at the murder site?"

I considered answering his question with a resounding no, but as Helmut had told me that he had lost his iPhone while attempting to revive his dead uncle, and I knew the detective would eventually prove the phone belonged to Helmut.

I said, "Detective Bauman, sometime ago I was informed by a man who lives in Carson

City that he had visited Nuremberg. Do you think it is possible the iPhone you found in the bookstore belonged to that man?"

"Herr Delmont, would you be able to provide me the name and address of the man who claimed to have lost his phone?"

"Detective, after he informed me that he lost his phone, I was retained as his attorney of record so any further discussions between my client and myself are protected under the attorney-client privilege."

"I understand. Herr Delmont, I have the distinct feeling that I have overstayed my welcome. Please allow me to give you my phone number. If you should ever have further contact with Helmut Kaufmann, please call me. One more item. If, by any chance, you should happen to come across the Achtliederbuch, please contact me at once me. That book is an essential part of the Kaufmann murder investigation, and as such, I will need it in Germany."

As I jotted down his number, I thought that he just gave me another reason for me to think the book was genuine. "Thank you, Detective Bauman, I will do that. Now, I have two final questions. Is Nuremberg the city where the Nazis rose to power prior to World War Two?"

"It is."

"And after we won the war, is it the same Nuremberg where the trials were held to prosecute and execute many of those Nazi war criminals who were found guilty?"

I detected a tone of something, almost an anger, in the detective's voice as he replied. "Mr. Delmont, you are correct on both statements."

"Detective Bauman, I wish you good luck finding the person, or persons, who caused the death of Konrad Kaufmann."

"Herr Delmont, just so you understand, my job is two-fold. First, to arrest the killer of Konrad Kaufmann. Second, on the wild chance that the book is authentic, return Martin Luther's Achtliederbuch to the the rightful owners, the people of Germany. You have my phone number. If you have any questions, or seek further clarification concerning the Kaufmann murder I am investigating, or the right of the German government to extradite an accused murder, I will be at your service. Wiedersehen."

Chapter Seven

Bear Zabarte—Carson City, Nevada

Flo was stuffing the vacuum cleaner into the closet when she said, "What was that last phone call all about?"

The infielders were throwing grounders to each other. "It was something about the boss wanting us to head to the Old Globe, pick up Helmut, and drive him somewhere. But for some reason he didn't tell me where or why."

"Helmut?"

The pitcher was taking his final warmup tosses to the plate. It was getting harder and harder to listen to Flo and watch the Sox game at the same time. "Like I said, Pinky didn't tell me why we have to pick up Helmut, so I guess it's not all that important."

I popped open a brew and sat back. Life doesn't get much better than this. A cold beer, my Bo-Sox on TV, and my babe's big boobs banging into my head. Hold on. Why are Flo's boobs banging into my head?

"Bear, swallow that mouthful of beer and then tell me what Pinky told you to do?"

"Something about picking up Helmut." I took another big swig of my beer, swallowed and said, "At The Old Globe I think, but he didn't tell me why. Hell, if it's up to me, I'd finish this game and then go pick him up."

"Damn it, Bear." She stomped over to the TV and ripped the plug out of the wall. The screen went black. "It doesn't make any difference what you want. Pinky's our boss, damn it. If he tells us to pick up Helmut we pick him up. Did he tell you a time?"

"Now that I think about it, he said like now."

Flo nodded. "I talked with Helmut a few days ago and it sounded like he's in deep shit again. That means you can't finish that damn baseball game. Get off your butt and let's go."

I could see there was no way to power up the TV with her holding the cord in her hand, so I set my beer down and lifted my butt out of my chair. "Okay, okay, Babe I'm up. What did Helmut do this time?"

Flo shook her head, walked to the front door and grabbed the keys to my truck out of the dish by the door. "You can ask him at the Old Globe."

I glanced back at the TV. The screen was darker than a skunk's butt. I knew if I tried to plug the damn thing back in my goose was cooked. I was pissed but I ran after Flo, took my keys out of her hand, jumped behind the steering wheel, and fired up the big V-8.

Five minutes later we walked into The Old Globe. I glanced around. It'd been a long time since I'd stood behind the bar, but nothing much had changed. The joint was a dive bar then, and it's still a dive bar. At the far end of the bar sat Helmut, nursing a beer.

I sat down on a bar stool next to him, reached over the bar, grabbed the TV remote and got the baseball game back on. "Helmut, how's it hanging?"

He took a sip of beer. "Not so good. Hello Flo."

I gave him a little punch on his arm. "Hey, where does Pinky want us to take you?"

"I don't know. He told me to give this envelope to Flo and she'd know what to do."

Helmut handed it to Flo. She opened it, read the note, and her face got all scrunched up, sort of like it would if a smelly old goat just walked by. She took her phone out of her purse and tried to talk quiet, like she didn't want us to hear, but I picked up most of her side of the call.

"Pinky, what the hell is wrong with you. We can't drive that far without some...but that's a...you're going to pay us an extra per diem to cover the...and we each get an additional clothing allowance!...Okay, you've got a deal…there's a key hidden in the flowerpot sitting by the front door?…Got it. And Bear'll call you on the land line when we get there."

Helmut didn't look like he was going to drink the rest of his beer so I downed it for him.

"Babe, are we going far enough to spend the night?"

"We are."

I wrapped my arms around her. "Hey, that sounds great. Where are we going?"

Flo shook her head. "I'll tell you later, after we're in the truck."

We were about ready to leave the bar when the door popped opened and a sheriff deputy walked in. He eyed me for a second, like he sorta recognized me, and then he headed toward the can. Back when I tended bar here, the fuzz were welcome to use the john cause the boss wanted the customers to know that any minute a cop might come cruising through the front door on his way to the crapper.

I still wasn't sure what Pinky was up to, but knowing that a cop could follow you was never a good idea. I whispered to Flo, "You two walk out of here giggling like you just got married. I'll check out the fuzz when he comes out of the john, and once the coast is clear, I'll meet you back at the truck."

Flo whispered, "I think we're okay. I'm pretty sure a federal extradition warrant would be served by a U. S. Marshal, not a deputy sheriff."

I whispered right back. "Extradition? U.S. Marshall? What the hell are we into?"

"Bear, forget I said anything."

"Babe, I may look stupid but I heard what you said about a U.S. Marshall serving a warrant. How do you know that the Federal dude ain't in cahoots with a sheriff deputy?"

She stared at me like I'd finally come up with something she hadn't thought of. "My God, you could be right."

Flo grabbed Helmut's hand and as they walked to the front door she yelled back to the bartender, "Charlie, thanks for the complimentary champagne wedding toast. We're heading over to the motel where I'm going to turn my new hubby every way but off."

Even dorky old Helmut got into the game. "Oh boy, I can hardly wait."

While I waited for the cop to come out of the can, I watched my Sox pitcher strike out the side, but before my guys came up to bat, the door to the can opened and he walked out. He didn't give me a second look, nodded to the bartender, and left through the front door.

I counted to thirty and followed him. The bright sun damn near blinded me, but I saw the cop's car pull away from the curb and head toward the east side of town. I joined Flo and Helmut who had ducked behind my truck. Before we jumped in, I told Helmut he had to sit on the back seat behind the driver, where you usually stick a kid or a dog. After he got in, me and Flo climbed into the front.

Flo said, "I think we're in the clear, but just in case, I'll monitor my sideview mirror to be sure nobody's following us."

"Babe, where are we headed?"

Flo shook her head, like all of a sudden she didn't trust me. "Just head south on 395."

"Gotcha."

After a couple of blocks, Flo stopped glancing at the sideview mirror and sat back. "No cop cars behind us. Okay, turn right when you get to the Highway 50 intersection and head up the hill."

"We're going to Tahoe?"

Helmut said, "Yes, I'd also like to know where we're going."

Flo checked the mirror again. "We're taking Helmut to one of Pinky's out-of-state condos."

I frowned, "Not Pinky's condo on the California side of the lake. The cops know all about that joint. Don't you remember? That's where we stuck Helmut last time."

"We're not going to Pinky's condo at Tahoe. Keep your mind on driving. We've got a long way to go."

Flo's always ragging on me how I don't use my brain for anything but baseball and beer and usually she's right. But for some dumb reason, as I headed west out of Nevada, our kid, Em, popped into my head.

Ettamae, or the Kid as I used to call her, wasn't really our kid. Hell, me and Flo ain't even married! But five to ten ears ago, that little girl I first spotted at her grandpa's motel on the Russian River, had somehow figured out how to weasel her way into our lives. Then her grandpa up and kicked the bucket so the Kid was a real orphan. I mean, if me and Flo hadn't jumped in, Ettamae would have been shipped off to some kind of orphanage or foster home.

That didn't sound good to me 'cause when I grew up in Elko, with a real mom and pop, I had somebody I could talk to when the shit hit the fan. I'm pretty sure a kid in an orphanage, or foster home, wouldn't have that.

So Ettamae moved in with me and Flo in Carson City. We didn't adopt her 'cause Flo was worried the State wouldn't let us 'cause we weren't married. So we're not Ettamae's real mom and pop but, after all these years, we might as well be. Anyway, the Kid grew up. One day, when she was a teenager, while eating Lucky Charms, her favorite cereal, the Kid stopped chewing and slammed her spoon onto the table. She told me that I had to stop calling her the Kid. Flo jumped in and said we'd hash this out during a family meeting. Shit, I really hate family meetings. So after the Kid got home from school that afternoon we all sat down. The damned family meeting took so long that I emptied four cans of brew while the Kid told Flo and me that she had never liked her real name, Ettamae. She thought the name was old fashioned, or something. So she took the E from Etta, and the M from Mae, and told us from that day on her new handle was Em. Then the Kid looked me square in the eye. She told me that now that she had a name she liked, Em, I had to stop calling her Kid and Flo agreed with her! Shit, I had called her Kid for so long that rooting for the damn Yankees woulda been easier. But by the time she graduated from high school she was Em to me. Now Em lives in Vegas where she goes to college.

By this time I was shooting past a big rig loaded with coffins from Indiana, I asked Flo, "Don't you think we oughta call Em and let her know we'll be out of town for a couple of days?"

"What's Em got to do with where we spend the night? She busy at school. I'll bet you ten

69

bucks she doesn't care where we are at this moment."

"Maybe so, but what if she runs out of cash, or falls down and hurts herself?"

"Bear, I've never quite figured you out concerning Em. Ever since we met her after you damn near drowned in that Russian River flood, there've been times when you treated her like your long-lost daughter, and other times you act like she's just another giant pain-in-the-ass. As far as I'm concerned, Em's our nineteen-year-old daughter who we've raised properly and she's old enough to take care of herself."

"Babe, I know all that, but—"

"No buts! She's a freshman at the University of Nevada in Las Vegas. Em has her circle of friends along with her own bank account."

"Hey, I know all about her bank account! That's where we keep stuffing money in every time she needs more dough." I clammed up when I spotted some real tears, not like her usual phony tears in the corners of Flo's eyes. Em was always a lot closer to Flo than she was to me, but that was okay 'cause I knew that all the babes sorta stick together. "You know, Flo, there are days when I actually miss Em."

Flo grabbed a Kleenex and blew her nose. "I miss her too."

I said, "Okay, so we both miss her."

Flo blew her nose again.

Helmut yelled, "Heads up, Bear, that truck in front looks like it's slowing down."

Shit, that's all I needed to make my day; a blubbering Babe, and a backseat driver.

Chapter Eight

Pinky Delmont—Carson City, Nevada

Before I had time to get upset with my present situation, Holly arrived.

An hour later I received a call from Loomer and he informed me that he had been unable to find a temporary to cover my office needs and he would instruct Holly to remain at her post until he could find my permanent replacement.

A moment later Holly received a phone call from Loomer with the identical information.

The expression of dismay on Holly's face informed me that she was not happy with that news and during the following hours I was forced to quell a few minor rebellions with my temporary replacement, but as usual, I ended up the victor.

The day after Holly's arrival, I was standing next to her desk, berating her over what I considered to be another grievous error on her part when the street-entrance door to my office crashed open. I glanced up and watched the front wheels of what I presumed to be a wheelchair enter halfway and then stop.

Holly, visibly relieved by the interruption, called out, "Welcome to the law office of J. Pincus Delmont."

As the wheels rolled over the threshold, a male voice bellowed, "Is Attorney Delmont in?"

I fired back, "That is I. And who are you?"

"Robert V. Silva. Excuse me, but do you have a bathroom?"

Holly said, "Yes, Mr. Silva, the restroom is through the door on your right."

But before Mr. Silva reached the lavatory door, I cried, "Mr. Silva, that restroom is not a public facility. It is for employee use only."

His powerful upper torso stopped propelling his chair toward the door. "Mr. Delmont, while I am your new legal secretary—a de facto employee if you like—but an employee none the less! Now, if you will excuse me."

He opened the door, deftly spun the chair around, backed in, and slammed the door shut.

I grabbed Holly's phone and punched in Loomer's number.

"Rapid Replacement. You find the need and we fill it!"

"Loomer. How dare you send me a man who is obviously recovering from some sort of ailment?"

"Pinky, Mr. Silva is not recovering from an illness. He's a paraplegic, who due to an unfortunate motor vehicle accident, has lost the use of his lower limbs. The man is a highly qualified legal secretary, and lucky for you, recently moved to Carson City from San Francisco so he is totally unaware of your reputation as a difficult boss. He told me between the steep hills and the traffic in San Francisco, going to work placed his very life at risk."

Before I could respond, the door to the bathroom opened and Mr. Silva's voice boomed out. "Mr. Delmont, this bathroom is in violation of the Americans with Disabilities Act passed by Congress in 1990. That law outlines, among many other items, disabled bathroom requirements. Those requirements include the dimensions of disabled bathrooms and the specialize equipment that those bathrooms must contain."

I said, "Loomer, I'll call you back!"

As I handed the phone to Holly, I said, "Mr. Silva, I understand your concern, but as you are the first disabled person to use that bathroom, I must point out that—"

Mr. Silva interrupted, "Accessible bathrooms for the disabled must have enough room to provide a turning space for a wheelchair. The toilet must be approachable by a wheelchair from the side or the front. Horizontal grab bars must be provided at the back of the toilet and on the nearest wall. Mr.

Delmont, as you can plainly see, I am a disabled person. I fully understand that you are, as are most Americans, totally ignorant concerning the ADA regulations. However, a qualified plumber should be able to bring this bathroom up to federal ADA standards within a few hours. I have been informed that you are in immediate need of a legal secretary, and, according to Mr. Loomer, I can assume those duties this afternoon. However, if the bathroom has not been brought up to ADA standards by five p.m. tomorrow, I will report your failure to the federal authorities.

As to my work schedule, I work Monday through Friday with weekends off. I will be at my desk no later than eight each morning, and will receive two twenty-minute breaks during each work day, one at ten and the second at two. My mid-day repast will begin at noon and last one hour. Finally, I will leave my desk at five each day. Are we in agreement, Mr. Delmont?"

I did not like anything this officious lout had said, but I required a legal secretary. As with everything in life, you have to know when to hold 'em, and know when to fold 'em, so I replied, "Yes, we are."

"Excellent, I'm ready to go to work."

I glanced at Holly and snapped, "Don't just sit there with your mouth open, find me a plumber who can bring that damn bathroom up to ADA standards. And once you have found a craftsman to do the job, as Mr. Silva will be taking over your desk, you are free to return to Rapid Replacement."

I turned and marched into my inner sanctum where I poured myself three-fingers of my excellent single malt. For a moment I smothered my angst with the Celtic elixir, but then I cursed Lu for walking out on me. My anger spiked as I recalled Louis Loomer and his damned contract plan. And Florence, yes, Florence! In the past I had successfully used her as my insurance policy in times of a dire office emergency. And where was she during this time of extreme need? Reveling in my Pacific Grove condo just minutes away from the soft sand at Asilomar beach, as if her personal comfort was more important than the well-being of her employer!

Chapter Nine

Bear Zabarte—on Highway 50

Between dodging the big-rigs, I glanced down at the gas gauge. "Babe, we shoulda filled up the tank in Carson City 'cause gas is a lot cheaper in Nevada."

"Don't worry about the price of gas. Pinky's paying for it."

"Okay, so I'll pull into the next gas stop."

Helmut said, "Florence, are we going to spend the night? I didn't bring my toothbrush."

I chimed in. "Or any toothpaste. Come on, Babe, where are we going?"

She stared out the front windshield for a couple of seconds, like she was sure if she didn't spill the beans pretty soon, I was going to get pissed off.

"Pacific Grove."

I'm pretty good at knowing where most of Nevada's towns are, even the little ones, 'cause I was born and raised in Elko in Eastern Nevada. And I know where a pot load of the California towns show up on a map, like L. A., and San Francisco, but I'd never even heard of Pacific Grove.

"Flo," said Helmut. "Is Pacific Grove that little town next to Monterey."

I barked, "Hey you two. I'm the dude holding the wheel of this damn truck and I still don't have a clue if we're headed in the right direction."

"Calm down, Bear, you just keep driving west on Highway 50. You'll pass Sacramento, and then we'll cross the San Joaquin Valley. Eventually, we'll end up near the ocean in Pacific Grove, about four hours from now."

Now I get why she clammed up on me. "Four hours? By then my baseball game'll be over."

"I'm sorry, but there'll be no more TV baseball games until Helmut is safely tucked away in Pinky's Pacific Grove condo."

"But Babe, this is the first game of the playoffs. If the Sox win the playoffs, then they go against the winner of—"

She sighed. "Stop right there. We've been through all this before. If you miss this one game your world won't come to an end."

"Hey, that's not the way baseball works. Like I told you, this is an important playoff game and every pitch—"

She slammed her elbow into my ribs. "Like I told you before, watching baseball on TV doesn't exist for you until we get Helmut inside Pinky's condo in Pacific Grove."

"Babe, I thought you liked baseball."

She smiled. "I do, but we work for Pinky, the guy who pays our bills. When he gives us a job to do, we have to do it!"

I'd known the boss a lot longer than she had, like I knew tons of the chicken-shit stuff he'd done, so when Pinky says jump I don't automatically ask how high. And I was pretty sure that my Babe does a whole lot less chicken-shit stuff than Pinky and I want to keep her on my side. So, it was time for me to cool it about watching baseball.

I said, "Babe, me and you are just like Helmut, we don't even have toothbrushes."

She said, "Don't worry. Pinky told me he will transfer $150 a day into our checking account to cover food costs while the three of us are in Pacific Grove, plus more expense money for some new clothes and toothbrushes."

If I know my Babe, and I do know my Babe, the bucks Pinky coughed up for new clothes was a lot more important to her than the hundred and fifty clams we get to buy grub.

"So you're telling me that I can buy me some new skivvies?"

She said, "God knows you need them. In fact, we will all receive a substantial clothing allowance."

"Babe, I don't know what substantial means. All I need is some clean skivvies, a pair of jeans, and a couple of tee shirts."

"Perfect. That will leave me more so I can buy some good-looking outfits," said Flo.

"I'm sure whatever me and Helmut don't spend on duds, you'll figure out a way to use it."

"Based on your fashion taste," Flo fired back. "A hundred bucks will cover the both of you."

"And I'll bet more than ninety-nine percent of the dudes in the world are the same."

The traffic on Highway 50 was light, but the big rigs that zigged and zagged between the lanes kept me on my toes. Don't get me wrong. I know a couple of dudes who bust their kidneys wrangling those big rigs, but those trucks went really, really slow on the upgrades. Then the damn things sometimes blocked two lanes on long downgrades 'cause they couldn't ride their brakes or they'd burn 'em out.

After I passed another slow-moving big rig, I said, "Babe, with all this talk about food, money, and new clothes, I didn't really get to ask my big question. Did you ask Pinky if there's a big screen TV at his condo? If not, I can drop you and Helmut off and head back to Carson City so I can watch the rest of the playoffs in peace."

Flo exploded. "You and your damned Red Sox!"

I could see that I had pushed the baseball thing a little too far and it was time for me to give her some time to simmer down.

For thirty minutes or so we just cruised past trees, rocks, cabins, mountain streams, and more damn trucks on our way down the mountain toward Sacramento. Then I spotted a sign for Placerville and took the first offramp to get gas. I said, "Babe, Helmut, this'll be our last stop 'til we get to Pacific Grove so you might want to make a pitstop to take a piss?"

Flo shook her head. "Bear, you have such a genteel way of phrasing things. I'll be right back so don't leave without me."

As Helmut ran toward the john, he called over his shoulder. "Me too."

After I paid for the gas, I headed to the can. After I'd finished my business, I went back into the store to buy three giant cups of coffee.

Before I started the truck, I handed the receipts to my Babe 'cause she puts all that crap in a special section of her purse so we have proof of our expenses in case that cheap boss of ours complains.

Speaking of our cheap boss, one of the few good things I learned from him was whenever the going gets tough, change the subject, so instead of griping about missing the game I set my hand onto Flo's knee. "Babe, do you think Pinky's right about the Feds being after Helmut?"

Flo put her hand on top of mine, a move that told me everything was okay now. "I'm afraid so."

Flo turned toward the back seat. "Helmut do you want to tell Bear how you got yourself into this mess?"

Helmut said, "I'm sorry you're suddenly involved in this unfortunate situation. It all started with my uncle's death."

I said, "Sorry to hear the old dude kicked the bucket."

"He was elderly, but that's not the reason he's dead."

Flo said, "Helmut, Bear knows you're in some sort of trouble. How bad is it?"

"The German police think I murdered my uncle."

My gut tightened, sort of like it does when I know there's more shit to hit the fan and I don't have the time to duck. "Murder? Jesus! Come on Helmut, its just me and Flo in this truck. Did you bump him off?"

Flo plowed her elbow into my side so hard I damn near changed lanes. "Babe, that hurt."

Flo flashed me one of her nasty stares "Hush." Then she turned toward Helmut. "I think I get it now. Is Pinky trying to avoid extradition?"

Helmut started to shake, like he was freezing, but it wasn't that cold. "I think so and that's what scares me. I can't spend the rest of my life in a German prison, but I also don't want to live the rest of my life hiding out in one of Pinky's condos."

As we shot past Sacramento, Helmut blurted out the whole enchilada. Like how he found the body, and then skedaddled out of Germany as fast as his feet could go.

When he was done, I was glad everybody shut up for a couple of minutes while I tried to figure out what to say to Helmut. Even though we went to the same high school in Elko, he was turning out to be one of the dumbest dudes I knew. Finally I said, "Okay, at least we all know why we're going to Pacific Grove."

Helmut said, "Pinky hinted that I had to do disappear, otherwise the Feds would get me and turn me over to the Germans."

Flo turned to me and flashed me her we-could-be-in-deep-shit looks. "Bear, I don't like what's going on here. If a cop pulls us over with Helmut riding in our truck, we could be charged with aiding and abetting a criminal."

Helmut stopped sniveling long enough to yell, "But Flo, you're not helping a criminal. I didn't murder my uncle!"

Flo said, "Calm down, you're preaching to the choir. Now everybody clam up so I can think." She laid her good-lookin' head back and closed her eyes.

Helmut didn't know how lucky he was to have a babe as smart as Flo in his corner. While she was trying to come up with something, I said, "Helmut, what do you think the odds are that the Red Sox'll get to the World Series?"

He didn't answer for a second, like the dude didn't have a clue. "Sorry, Bear, I'm not a fan of baseball."

"Oh!"

Flo sat up and pulled the phone out of her purse. "I'm going to call Pinky."

She tapped the screen and before Lu answered, she hit the speaker phone button. After the second ring, we all heard a dude's voice say, "Law Office of J. Pincus Delmont. How may I help you?"

I said, "Hey, who are you? And why are you answering Lu's phone? Put Lu on or get me Pinky."

"To answer your first question, my name is Robert V. Silva. My response to your second query is I answered this phone because I work for attorney Delmont, and part of my assigned duties, as I understand them, are to answer the office telephone when it rings. Concerning your third issue, Attorney Delmont is currently unavailable. Finally, there is no one here named Lu. Would you care to leave a message?"

This dude sure knew how to piss a guy off in ten seconds or less. Only Pinky would hire a temp that has the personality of a rattlesnake. "Dude, I'm driving west on Highway 50 with Flo and Helmut and we need to talk with Pinky, like right now."

"To whom am I speaking?"

"Bear."

"Excuse me? Is that really your name?"

Jesus, what a dork. "Yes it is. I'm Bear, Bear Zabarte."

"As I previously stated Mr. Zabarte, Attorney Delmont is out. If you do not care to leave a message, then I recommend you hang up and find someone else to pester."

Flo pulled the phone away just before I told that dip shit where he could stick my message. She said, "Mr. Silva, my name is Florence. Bear and I both work for Pinky as his investigative team. Please understand our ignorance because up to a few hours ago the person who answered Pinky's phone was a woman named Lu. I'm sure that will help you understand Bear's confusion."

"Ms. Florence, I appreciate that you explained the reason for your call, but as I previously explained to that other person,

85

unless you care to leave a message, I am unable to assist you. Is there anything else I can help you with?"

I could see that Flo was so pissed off she was about to throw my phone out the window.

I said, ""Dump the call Babe."

And she did!

Chapter Ten

Pinky Delmont—Carson City, Nevada

My intercom buzzed. I said, "Yes?"

Robert said, "You have a caller on line one by the name of Willow. Pinky, as I am new to your office, I need to know if you wish to receive her calls in the future."

"Affirmative, Robert. Willow is my favorite ex-wife and as such—"

Robert cut me off mid-sentence. "Thank you, I believe that's more information than I require. Also, while you were out getting your hair cut, I received a call from a couple calling themselves Bear and Florence. Do you wish to continue to receive their calls?"

"Also affirmative. They are my investigative team."

"I'm sure they are. Thank you."

I glanced at my watch and noted it was nearly two. I pushed the button for line one. "Willow, my sweet. I am pleased that you called me back, but it is a little late for us to make our lunch reservation in Reno."

"Pinky, I was ready almost two hours ago. When I called you back no one answered the phone. After six or seven rings I hung up.

Damn it, Pinky, that's the last time you'll stand me up."

"My love, you cannot believe the morning I've experienced. I had an appointment to get my hair cut, then Lu just vanished and then—"

"Pinky, I don't care about your morning, or about your haircut, or what happened with Lu. You asked me to call you back and then someone, if Lu was gone, I assume that person was you, refused to answer my return call. Then you didn't have the courtesy to call me back to apologize. Listen to me, your lack of civility today is the last straw. You and I are through. I've already changed the number on my personal cell line and told my receptionist not to accept any calls from you on my office line. Goodbye!"

The phone went dead before I could open my mouth. Shocked at the thought of never seeing the love of my life again, I turned, pulled out my bottle of whiskey and poured a full five fingers into a glass. After I downed the amber liquid, I walked out of my office, glanced at Robert and instinctively knew that he was not the person to discuss personal problems with. Determined to overcome my latest rebuff, I left the office and strolled around the park-like setting that fronted the Nevada Legislature building.

To my surprise, I spotted a hot dog stand at the corner of Fifth Street and Highway 395.

"What can I get for you?" asked the vendor.

"I bought one of the best hot dogs I ever ate from this very stand when I first moved to Carson City. Do you still offer those great hot dogs?"

"I do."

"I will take a hot dog and a sparkling water."

"You've got it."

That hot dog was all it took. Much of the pain of my sudden breakup with Willow remained, but my legendary reserve of resiliency helped me recover from my momentary low. After my lunch in the clean fresh air, I returned to my office, sat back, and reviewed the notes of my conversations with Detective Bauman. Without question, the Germans had a solid case against my client.

As I began to consider a potential defense strategy, I reminded myself that my action to help Helmut Kaufmann avoid extradition could make me an accessory after the fact. But as long as Helmut remained hidden, I was safe.

However, the more I considered my legal vulnerability, I feared that sooner or later even my perfect plan could fail. Helmut might get cabin fever, be captured, extradited to

Germany, and I could be charged with obstruction of justice for hiding him.

At this point, the only way out of what might turn out to be a very sticky situation for me, was to send Florence and Bear to Nuremberg to see if they could come up with a second suspect, someone with a motive, means, and opportunity to murder Konrad Kaufmann.

Realizing that time was not on my side, I pulled out one of the 'burner' cell phones from my desk and dialed the landline at my condo in Pacific Grove.

Florence answered on the second ring.

"Florence, now that you have Helmut safely ensconced, I have another assignment for you two."

"Before you go on, could Bear and I be charged with aiding and abetting a criminal for driving Helmut to Pacific Grove?"

"No. That's a common misconception."

She said, "Thank heavens. I was worried."

"Although it is possible that you two could be charged under the accessory after the fact statute."

"Damn you, Pinky. I had a gut feeling you'd get us into legal trouble on this one. I'm going to put the rest of this call on speaker so Bear can hear."

"Florence, stop talking and listen to me. I have a solution concerning any possible accessory after the fact charges against you and Bear. First, you need to go out and buy enough food so Helmut can stay out of the public eye for at least a month. Next, you and Bear will be flying to—"

Bear growled, "Hold it right there, Boss. I thought we were supposed to be babysitting Kaufmann? Why do we have to go—""

"Nuremberg, Germany. I need to find out if Konrad Kaufmann could have had a first edition of the Achtliederbuch in his bookshop."

Bear yelled, "Actor, what?"

"The Martin Luther Hymnal, you dolt. Florence, after I finish this call, please explain to Bear what you and I have previously discussed concerning the possible existence of a first edition of the Achtliederbuch. Now, are we on the same page?"

Bear said, "Boss, I still don't have a clue what the hell you're talking about. I hope Flo does."

Flo said, "Except for the fact that I don't agree with you that a first edition of the Achtliederbuch exists, I guess we're on the same page. Move on."

I said, "To get Helmut out of this sticky situation we need to come up with another suspect, and to accomplish that task you and Bear will fly to Nuremberg, Germany. Once there, you need to find someone who had the motive, means, and the opportunity to murder Konrad Kaufmann."

Bear said, "Boss, let me get this straight. We fly to Germany to find a patsy, and then we frame him so the German cops think that the patsy, not Helmut, murdered his uncle. Right?"

That was exactly what I meant, but I would never admit that to another living being, much less Bear and Florence. "Bear, quiet down and listen to me. As soon as I hang up, I will instruct Robert to make your travel arrangements and provide Florence with a two-thousand-dollar advance against your expenses. Florence, if your cash advance drops to five hundred dollars, contact Robert and he will arrange to advance you more funds. Now, I have a court appearance that I have to make."

Bear said, "Boss, any ideas on what we should do once we land in kraut land?"

"Yes, contact the man in charge of the Kaufmann murder investigation. His name is Detective Bauman. He is your man once you find the new suspect. I put his phone number on the note I passed on to Florence. Any further question?"

"Hold on, let me check the note," said Florence. "Okay, I've got the phone number. Now, I have a bone to pick with you before we agree to this German investigation."

"And what is that?"

"Today, without our knowledge, you put Bear and me at risk of being arrested as accessories after the fact! When I woke up this morning, I did not plan on being thrown in jail because you directed me to commit a crime. Pinky, your indiscretion is going to cost you."

Between the German detective, Lu walking out, Robert V. Silva, the damned ADA bathroom laws, Willow leaving me, and now Florence's demands, I had been stripped of the energy required to argue with her. "Florence, without agreeing that I placed either of you in any legal danger, what sort of cost am I going to incur?"

"Inform Robert that Bear and I are flying business class to Nuremberg."

"What!"

"And be sure he understands those business class reservations are round trip."

I jumped up and started to pace around my desk to defuse my anger. "Florence, I will do no such thing. You are fully aware that my investigative team always flies coach class, and only coach class, while on assignment."

"Not this trip! Hey, if you don't want us to go to Germany that's fine with me. Pacific Grove is a lovely place to spend some much-needed vacation time. Although it's foggy, I'm sure that's temporary, and Asilomar beach is only a block away. Before you called, Bear and

I were about to change into our bathing suits and head to the sand."

I considered calling her bluff, but I wasn't one hundred percent sure that she was bluffing. I needed them in Germany to come up with a valid suspect for the Kaufmann murder. I said, "Agreed. But this trip does not constitute a change in my standard policy concerning air fare. After your German assignment, coach class will be your mode of air transport. Do we understand?"

"Pinky, just as long as we're flying business class to and from Nuremberg, Bear and I will do your dirty work."

"Florence, one moment." I set the cell phone down. Poured myself the last of the single malt that remained in the bottle. I downed half the glass and picked the cell phone back up. "Then we are in agreement. Business class to and from Nuremberg. Coach class after that."

"Pinky, if saying those words makes you feel better, so be it. We'll stop by your office tomorrow to say goodbye before we take off."

Chapter Eleven

Flo Sunderlund—In the air between Reno and Nuremberg, Germany

Bear asked me to take over his job of recording the following events because the bottom line is my man's afraid of flying— anywhere, anytime—much less flying from Reno to Paris with a connecting flight to Nuremberg. No, my man was not up to taking notes while he was trapped for many, many hours inside a giant metal tube, flying 30,000 feet above the ground, at more than 500 miles per hour, to complete the 6,000 mile flight between Reno and Nuremberg.

So how did I get him to not care about where he was going and how long it was going to take him to get there? The same method I used a year ago when we flew from Copenhagen to San Francisco. I asked the flight attendant to bring us each two beers. After she left, I gave Bear my two beers along with two melatonin pills. He downed the pills, along with the four beers, and just like clockwork, before our plane was over Salt Lake

City, Bear was snoring like an overworked chainsaw.

Once he had drifted off to la la land, I started to read my book on Martin Luther by Eric Metaxas. After my course on the Reformation during college, I thought I knew everything I needed to about Martin Luther between his brith in1483 and his death in 1546. However, by the time we were over the Atlantic Ocean, I began to understand just how much that man had changed the world as we know it today.

I almost woke Bear up when the attendant served a tasty breakfast of scrambled eggs, bacon, warm sourdough toast, and hot coffee. Another perk of business class. But I was careful to eat quietly and other than a few snorts and honks, he slept through me eating breakfast.

When we were about thirty minutes from landing in Paris, I woke Bear up. As usual, he was surprised to discover that he had slept for that long and all he wanted to do was, to use his terminology, "Throw some water on my face, take a piss, and find some grub."

After a few minutes in the restroom, Bear hunted down our attendant and asked her when breakfast was going to be served. she followed him to his seat with a tray of food.

After he clicked his seat belt, she set the tray down and whispered, "I'm not supposed to be serving any food this late but don't worry, I'll be back to pick up what you don't eat before we land."

Obviously, the attendant didn't know Bear as well as I did because when she stopped by to pick up the tray, he had eaten everything but the plastic plates, knives, forks, and spoons.

By the time the plane's wheels touched the asphalt at De Gaulle Airport, my man was happy, rested, well fed, and ready for the short connecting flight to Nuremberg.

Chapter Twelve

Bear Zabarte—Nuremberg, Germany

In a little more that an hour after we landed in Paris, we boarded another plane to Nuremberg and not much more than sixty minutes later, the plane touched down in Nuremberg. While the plane was rolling on the ground, I asked Flo, "Babe, got any ideas how we're going to come up with a local patsy that the German cop would fall for?"

She said, "I don't have a clue. But one thing I'm pretty sure about is that we'll have to find a genuine suspect because we can't assume that the German cops are incompetent. Pinky told me that the detective he talked with sounded sharp and seemed to know what he was doing."

"Don't worry, Babe, I've got a plan. Just follow my lead."

She frowned. "I thought you were sleeping the past eight hours. Just what is this plan?"

"I'll get that German cop thinking I'm nothing but a dumb hick from Nevada. That's where you come in. You know, he'll show us around the murder scene and tell us how great a job he's doing. But all that time he'll be thinking about what a beautiful babe you are and forget all about me."

Flo smiled, "Bear, being a dumb hick from Nevada is the perfect disguise for you."

I was pretty sure she was putting me on, but I didn't care. The plane was on the ground and that was the most important thing to me right now. "Babe, if you keep giving the detective a smile every now and then he might forget who you are and tell you what kind of a case they have on Helmut"

Flo said, "I think it's a stretch, but it's better than anything I've come up with."

After a couple more minutes the plane finally stopped moving and people jumped up, like they wanted to be the first dudes to get out the door.

As we left the plane, I said, "You know, finding a patsy doesn't scare me as much as being in a country where everybody talks German. How am I going to understand anything?"

"Don't worry Bear, most Germans speak English better than you do."

I think she just zapped me again but I didn't care 'cause at that point I was too hungry to argue. That cute babe on the plane with the perky boobs had brought me a few bran muffins with some coffee, but some dinky muffins were more like a snack than a real breakfast.

I grabbed our bags from the carousel and was standing in line to get our passports stamped when a guy wearing a gray cop uniform walked up, grabbed my arm, and started to pull me out of the line.

I pushed him away. "Dude, I don't give a damn that you're dressed up like a cop. You've got ten seconds to get your mitts off me, or I'm going to smack you one square on the nose."

Just then an older guy wearing a regular suit moved between me and the cop. He whispered something to the uniform and the cop let go of my arm.

As soon as the fuzz backed off, the suit flashed me and Flo a smile. "Good morning. My name is Detective Joseph Bauman of The Bavarian State Police. Herr Delmont emailed me that you would be arriving on this flight from Paris and I wanted to be the first to welcome you to Germany and our fine city of Nuremberg."

Damned if Flo wasn't right about the Germans speaking English. This old dude looked German. Like twenty years ago his almost white hair was blonde, along with steely blue eyes, and a nose sort of hacked out of a chunk of marble. And just like she said, the German suit spoke better English than me.

Flo said, "If you'll excuse me, Detective Bauman, I just spotted the ladies restroom."

As my babe skedaddled across the hall, I shoved my hand in the suit's direction but he didn't move, so I figured that Germans can speak English but they don't shake hands like we do in America.

While we waited for my Babe, I gave the dude a second once over. He was over six feet tall and for an old fart he had a pretty buff body, like he must work out a lot. And his suit looked like it cost as much as one of Pinky's Italian imports. One time, Pinky told me that his suits cost him over a thousand clams each, so German cops must make more bucks than American cops do. And that's another thing. I know the Germans don't use bucks, clams, or dollars. Hell, I don't know what they call their German money. But I do know that I've never figured out why a dude would spend a thousand clams for clothes when he can get three pair of the best Levis for less than two hundred bucks at JC Penneys.

I said, "Thanks for taking care of that uniformed fuzz. I don't know what Pinky told you, but me and Flo are here to nose around where the bookstore dude got murdered and—"

"Herr Zabarte, I have a feeling that you and your partner are in Nuremberg to find someone to take the place of Helmut Kaufmann as my prime suspect. I commend your efforts in advance. I will assist you in any way I can, but you need to understand, that in my opinion, Helmut Kaufmann is the one and only possible suspect for the murder of his uncle, Konrad Kaufmann. My main objective at this point in my investigation is the extradition of Helmut Kaufmann. I realize that at this moment Helmut Kaufmann is missing, but once we find him, and we will find him, he will be brought back to Germany where he will be put on trial for murder."

I was glad that this German dude didn't pull any punches. Damn, I shoulda known Pinky wasn't going to send us on a vacation to Germany. Shit, how in the hell are we suppose to manufacture a patsy for the Kaufmann murder when the suit's pretty much knows that's why me and Flo are here? But one thing I picked up working for Pinky is when you don't know what to do next, bluff like you're the nastiest dude in the fight.

"Joe, I don't know anything about that extradition crap, but I do know that me and Flo have got a job to do."

The second I called him Joe, I noticed a little twitch in the wrinkles next to his right eye. A muscle jump like that is called a 'tell' to poker players. If we had any chance of clearing

Helmut, I had to figure out if Joe's muscle twitch was a real 'tell', or just a coincidence.

But first I'd better explain what a tell is 'cause this is when Flo usually jumps in to do that sort of thing. Since she's still in the babe's john, you're stuck with me, and trust me this is the straight skinny from a dude who's made some bucks playing poker. A tell is NOT a good thing to have if you're a poker player, 'cause if you've got a tell, all the other dudes sitting around the table will be watching for it,. Pretty soon, by seeing that tell, they'll know when you're bluffing.

I said, "Hey Joe, I need some help here. My hands are full. Can you grab Flo's suitcase?"

Damn, there's that same little twitch again. Now I was sure that he was getting pissed off when I called him Joe, so from now on I'll know when Joe's ticked off at anything I say or do.

I could see that Joe was working hard to stay calm, but he was barely holding it together. "Herr Zabarte, in the future, please address me as Detective Bauman."

Flo waltzed up just in time to hear me say, "Got it, Joe. I've heard you Germans like to be formal about that sort of name crap, but you're dealing with a high school graduate from Elko, Nevada, and where I come from we don't give a shit what another dude calls us, and visa-versa.

You know, you kinda remind of my boss, Pinky. He gets pissed off at me when I call him boss, so I do it on purpose 'cause I know it gets to him. So once and for all, let's me and you get this straight. My name is Bear. My babe's name is Flo. And we'll call you Joe. Got it?"

The suit looked like his white hair was about to catch fire when Flo stepped between us. "Herr Bauman, I know my man, and trust me, once Bear decides to call you Joe, it's all over. In fact, you should be happy he calls you Joe and not some other nasty name he could have come up with."

The German dude glanced at Flo and then backed off. "Herr Zabarte, I insist that—"

I interrupted, "Joe, come to think of it, there is one more thing you can do for me. I didn't get a real breakfast on the plane so I'm looking for a place where I can get some scrambled eggs along with a big chicken fried steak smothered with white, sausage gravy. After I eat, I'll probably be thirsty so maybe you could find us a decent hotel where I can eat breakfast, down a few brews, and then me and Flo can get some much needed shut-eye. Tomorrow morning, once we get our feet under us, you can stop by and show us around town."

The dude's jaw tightened up so much that I was afraid his teeth might weld together. Then he snapped to attention, and I swear on a stack of Bibles, just like those Nazis dudes did in those old war movies, his heels clicked when they came together. "Herr. . . pardon me. Bear, Flo, I have the perfect hotel for you in mind. They have a cafe that can serve you an American breakfast, and an excellent bar stocked with some of our finest German beers. My car is parked at the curb outside the terminal. Let me assist you with your luggage. We can be at your hotel in ten minutes."

Flo yawned, "That sounds good to me, Herr Bauman. My man can eat and drink all he wants, but I didn't didn't get any shut-eye during the flight. All I need is a soft place to rest my weary body."

Chapter Thirteen

Pinky Delmont—Carson City, Nevada

My intercom buzzed. I picked up the receiver and Robert said, "Pinky, you have a call waiting from someone who says her name is Lu. I tried to get her to give me a reason for her call, but she refused. Do want me to inform her that you are busy and screen any future calls?"

"No, I will talk to her." Before I picked up her call, I pondered why I should lower myself to talk with a former employee who had gone AWOL. After a moment of reflection, however, I decided to be magnanimous. "Hello, Lu. This is a pleasant surprise. What can I do for you?"

"Pinky, at this point you can do nothing for me. I tried to tell you that I was going to leave, but as usual, you were lost in your own egotistical world."

I didn't respond to her obvious taunt.

"Pinky? Are you still there?"

"My good woman, you have my complete attention."

"It's about time. Now, although you may not agree, I had a valid reason for leaving without notice. I received a phone call from the father of my child. He was flying from Boston to Reno and we were to be married soon after his plane landed."

Few situations catch me off guard, but I had to admit that Lu's unexpected marriage was one of those times. My mind raced with potential possibilities, nearly all of them negative. I leaned forward. "My dear, as my wedding gift to you, I am going to send you a check for one thousand dollars. It is not every day that one's majordomo gets married."

"Pinky, you can't alleviate your guilty conscious by sending me some of your ill-gotten gains. Now, for once, listen to me and don't interrupt. Originally, I was going to give you some notice. But after you couldn't bother to give me a few minutes of your valuable time to hear my story, I decided to move to Cape Cod immediately following the wedding."

I said, "Lu, I fully realize that we have had a few minor problems in the past, but—"

"I told you not to interrupt me. Pinky, you pushed me to the point that I couldn't take your misogynistic attitude any longer—the way you treat all women. Think about how you deal with your ex-wife, Willow, and Flo. That's the real reason I left!"

"Lu, I understand."

"No. I don't think you do."

I hesitated. "Then there's nothing I can do?"

"Nothing."

"Lu, business is business. Life moves on. By the way, you have already been replaced by an extremely efficient legal secretary. Now, if you will excuse me, I have a court date. Goodbye."

I slammed the phone down, spun my chair around and pulled out my bottle of single malt to pour myself four full fingers of my finest whiskey. To my surprise, the bottle was empty. Then I decided that a single phone call from Lu was nothing and placed the empty bottle back in my credenza. That simple act allowed my anger to subside as I buzzed Robert.

"Yes."

"Robert, I have decided that I cannot continue to address you by your full name. I'm sorry, but that must change. Did you have a nickname as a child or in school?"

"I did not."

"I find that hard to believe."

"Pinky, if you'll excuse me, I'm falling behind on my prescribed duties."

"Robert, it is obvious that my nickname, Pinky, comes from: Pincus. You must have a nickname, like Bob, or Robbie?"

"I told you not a moment ago, no nicknames. Is there anything else you need from me?"

"My good man, I have not asked you to divulge the combination to the gold reserves at Fort Knox."

"Pinky, listen to me. The accident that turned me into a paraplegic took more than my legs. My injury turned me into the bitter person who now works in a podunk town for lawyer, who I've been told, has questionable ethics."

At that point I regretted that I had brought up the nickname discussion. "Robert, you've strayed far beyond a simple discussion of nicknames. Fine, it will be Robert from now on. In the future, I will be "out of the office" to my ex-secretary Lu Yong. That includes phone calls, emails, text messages, snail mail, or personal visits. Oh, and when you have a free moment, take some money out of petty cash and replace the empty bottle of single malt sitting on my desk. That will be all."

As I pulled the empty bottle out of the credenza and placed it on my desk, I smiled. Robert will learn that occasionally I lose a few battles, but I always win the war.

Chapter Fourteen

Bear Zabarte—Nuremberg, Germany

I hated to admit it, but that nasty German cop, Joe, got us checked into a really cool hotel. Our room was large with a big soft bed. The cafe breakfast was great. And after I finished the grub, I moved to the bar where the bartender poured me a couple of mugs of great beer.

As usual, my Babe was right. The German's know how to make beer.

The next morning, after a long, hot shower with my babe, me and Flo headed downstairs to the breakfast buffet. The hotel laid out one of the best breakfast spreads I'd seen since we stayed at that Best Western in dumb Eureka, Nevada. While I was chowing down, Flo told me that a lot of Germans kicked off the day with a spread like that.

There were all kinds of sliced cheese, meat, different kinds of bread, little pots full of great jam, and lots of black coffee strong enough wake the dead.

I'd just finished wiping a glob of jam off my lower lip when Joe, the German cop in a suit walked through the door followed by a young dude who trailed behind him like he was a puppy dog on a leash.

"Guten morgen, Herr Bear and Frau Flo. I trust you both had a good night's rest?"

Me and Flo stood up from our table. "Joe, one of these days you've got to explain what somebody's hair's got to do with my name. Remember, I'm just Bear, right?"

With that, Joe's right eye started to twitch real hard. He said, "As you wish. And the Frau?"

Flo smiled. "Flo is just fine with me."

"I've got to hand it to you, Joe. You hit a home run with this joint. Nice bed, great breakfast, and a bar loaded with great beer. Got one complaint. Last night I couldn't find the Sox's game anywhere on TV. But that was okay last night 'cause Flo was trying to sleep. Now that we're done with breakfast I'll talk to that snooty dude who checked us in about where to find the game. I'll bet you a beer he'll come up with a way to get that ballgame into our room."

Joe gave me a long stare like he didn't have a clue what the hell I was talking about. Then he said, "I would like to introduce you to one of my staff, Juri Vogel. During your stay in Nuremberg, Juri will be your companion."

I glanced at the new dude. He was a good looking kid, probably in his late twenties. He was decked out in a suit and tie, like his boss, but his slicked-down hair was light brown, not blond. His face was sorta tan, like he spent a lot of time at the beach. And his eyes were brown, like his hair. Even I could tell that Juri didn't look as German as his boss, Joe. In fact, he looked like his mom, or dad, came from some other country, like my Pop who came from the Basque part of Spain.

Obviously, Joe wasn't going to waste his time showing me and Flo around Nuremberg. Remembering what Joe told me yesterday, I was pretty sure Juri wasn't just a tour guide. His main job was to stick with us and report back all our moves to his boss. Like how many brews I downed a day to how often I farted. I sorta smiled in Juri's direction.

Flo, who was usually a hell of a lot nicer to strangers than I was, said, "Juri, your last name Vogel translates to bird in English. Am I correct?"

"Ja, Frau Flo."

I said, "Stop right there, Juri, it's like I told your boss, Joe. I'm just Bear, and she's just Flo. Got it?"

The young dude stared at me for a second and then looked at his boss.

Joe said, "Verwenden Sie nicht Herr und Frau. Und nur Englisch sprechen."

"Ich werde das tun."

I almost screwed up and asked Flo what they just said, but at that point in our visit she didn't want to let Joe, or Juri, know that she understood German. Like Joe might say something in German that they wanted to keep under their hat. So I said, "Joe, I don't have a clue what you two dudes just said, so I don't see how Juri's going to be our eyes and ears if we can't figure out what he's saying."

"I apologize, Bear. I just informed Juri not use Herr and Frau when addressing you. And that he should always speak English when talking to you."

"And what did he say?"

"He will do that."

I said, "Okay, Juri. Me and Flo want to head to the bookstore where the old dude bought the farm."

Juri said, "Excuse me, but there are no farms near the bookstore. In fact, we would have to drive out into the countryside to find you a farm."

Flo laughed. "Juri, 'bought the farm' is an English euphemism. What Bear meant to say was we want to go to the bookstore where Herr Kaufmann was found dead."

I said, "Flo's right on. The place where Kaufmann bought his pine condo."

Joe turned, like he suddenly had something more important to do. "I am sure Juri will take care of all your needs while you are in Nuremberg. Goodbye."

But just before Joe left, he grabbed Juri's arm and turned him around, so all we could see was their backs. Then, like a couple of pissed off junk-yard dogs, the two whispered barks back and forth in what sounded to me like a full-blown argument. Shit, I didn't know any German but whispering wasn't going to change the fact that those two dudes were hammering at each other. I hoped that Flo picked up most of what the two were squabbling about.

Once Joe left, I told Juri, "Me and Flo have got to head upstairs to our room. You know, to brush our teeth and stuff. We'll meet you in the lobby in fifteen minutes."

"I will be waiting for you by the front desk."

While we rode up in the elevator, I said, "Okay, what the hell was going on between those two?"

"Joe told Juri to take us to the site of the murder, and then show us around town. That's when the argument started. Juri felt he had to take us to the *Reichsparteitagsgelände.*"

"Jesus, what the hell is that?"

"I think the English translation would be Congress Hall. He also thought we should see one other place, *Zeppelinfeld.*"

"I guess we've got to go along with him, but none of that crap sounds very interesting. Is that all?"

"Not by a long shot. Then Joe closed with a direct order that Juri not bring up the neo-Nazi angle. I missed a little in the middle but picked up the rest of the argument when Joe emphatically stated that he's the boss of this investigation and Helmut Kaufmann is their one and only suspect."

"Neo-Nazis? Did that German dude actually say neo-Nazis?"

The elevator door opened and Flo said, "He did. I'll try to explain more later when we have a little more time."

"Babe, it's a good thing those dudes don't know that you understand German."

Flo smiled, just like she does when she pulls a fast one on Pinky. Then she said, "Do you think we'll find anything at the murder site that the cops missed?"

"Probably not, but it's our chance to get tight with Juri. He knows Nuremberg and he if he thinks somebody else might be a suspect for the old dude's murder then Juri's the guy to help us find a verbal patsy."

"I think you mean viable patsy instead of verbal patsy."

"Whatever. Don't forget, Babe, we only need to find one dude who had the means, motive, and opportunity. Thanks to you, we know that Juri and Joe don't agree 'bout how many suspects there are in this murder case. All we have to do is convince Juri to diss his boss and help us."

Suddenly, Flo stopped in the hall outside our room and grabbed my arm. "That's it! Something's been bugging me since we drove Helmut to Pacific Grove. He didn't have a motive to strangle his uncle. Remember? While we were driving past Sacramento, he told us that FedEx delivered a box that contained a book before he flew to Nuremberg."

"Damn, you're right! Helmut had the book before he flew to Germany. So why would he strangle his uncle? Great, I'll call Pinky and tell him we can get our plane tickets and we'll be on our way back home."

She frowned. "Hold on. First we've got to come up with a way to let Juri know that we know Helmut never had a motive. Remember, he had the book in his possession before he flew to Germany. Of course Helmut told us that while we were hiding him from extradition in Pinky's condo in Pacific Grove. Come to think of it, we never saw a copy of the book. However, we're pretty sure that Pinky has the book tucked away somewhere. Bear, tell me again. What are we going to accomplish going to the bookstore with Juri?"

"Babe, why do you keep coming up that sort of stuff? Hell, I was ready to hop a plane back to Carson City."

"But I thought you'd want to sample more of that great German beer before we fly home. Perhaps you can do that while I check out some of the sights in Nuremberg."

I was glad she reminded me about the beer. A couple more days here can't hurt, and what the hell, Pinky's paying for it. "Babe, try this one on for size. We've got to convince the young cop that he knows more than his boss, Joe."

"Good plan. Then what?"

"I don't know. but we'll come up with something." I glanced at my watch. "Hey, we've got damn near ten minutes before we've got to meet Juri downstairs. How about it, Babe do we have enough time to fool around?"

"We did that in the shower before breakfast. And besides, Juri's waiting for us in the lobby."

"I guess you're right. Babe, before we leave the hotel this morning, I'm going to talk to one of those dudes behind the counter to find out how he can get me the damn Red Sox game on the TV in our room."

Chapter Fifteen

Pinky Delmont—Carson City, Nevada

After a morning of turmoil, I decided to leave my office and head to the peace and quiet of home. But as I pushed my chair back from my massive mahogany desk, the FedEx box came into my thoughts. The little cardboard container that held either a worthless copy, or a priceless first edition of Martin Luther's Achtliederbuch.

I opened my safe, pulled out the box and considered my options.

If the book was a copy, what resided in the FedEx box had little or no value.

However, if the box I held in my hands contained a priceless first edition, I was ready to sell it to the highest bidder. But I had to careful. Martin Luther's Achtliederbuch was not the sort of item one would see at a standard Sotheby's auction.

To sell this book I had to find a private buyer. A collector who was not afraid to nibble around the edge of legality to buy a priceless antiquity. I would be seeking a buyer who purchased rare items not to display them, but to possess them.

But how does one go about finding that type of buyer? Suddenly I knew just the man who could answer that question.

I pushed the intercom button. "Robert, have you retained Lu's old Rolodex?"

"I have."

"Excellent. Find the phone number of a Mr. Dudek, He may be listed under Jake Dudek, or Hook Dudek. Once you get him on the line, let me know."

"Will do."

As I waited, a chill ran up my spine as I recalled my last association with Hook Dudek, an event that turned out to be extremely unpleasant. In fact, if I recall correctly, I had admonished Hook to never contact me again! He was to stay away from me and my office. And if he did not follow my exhortation, I would call the police and have them to arrest him as a stalker!

However, that earlier event took place nearly two years ago and much water had passed under the bridge since I last talked to the man with a sharp stainless-steel hook for a right hand.

My intercom buzzed. "Pinky, Mr. Dudek is on line one."

I pushed the button and said, "Ah, Mr. Dudek. It has been a while since we last talked."

"Shyster, how many times do I have to tell you. Hook is the name. I thought the last time we saw each other you told me to never darken your door again."

"Why, Hook, you must be mistaken."

"Hey, don't forget I know the real Pinky Delmont: the dude sitting next to me in a helicopter who had just pissed himself because some New Jersey Goombas were about to drop him a thousand feet into the cold Atlantic ocean."

My hand began to quiver as the mental picture of that near fatal helicopter ride over the Atlantic brought back memories I had worked hard to suppress.

Hook continued, "So don't think that you can dazzle me with your usual line of bullshit. But hey, what happened to us in New Jersey stays in New Jersey, right?"

I was pleased that Hook was on the other end of the phone line so he couldn't see me fighting to stop my hand trembling.

Hook continued, "Moving on, we both know you didn't call me to talk about the weather. I'm guessing it's a job but not something you want to discuss over the phone."

As my hands stopped shaking, I said, "You are correct. This is something we need to talk over in private."

"Pinky, do you still store that 25-year-old single malt in the credenza behind your desk?"

I was initially concerned that Hook knew where I hid my expensive whiskey, but then reminded myself that knowing where nearly all of Carson City's valuables were tucked away was Hook's raison d'être.

I said, "My good man, once we agree on a plan of attack, you and I will seal the deal with a glass of Scotland's finest."

"Pinky, as this has been a slow day for me, I'll stop by your office in fifteen minutes. 'Til then."

For a moment, I sat back and tried to imagine the mayhem that could possibly happen during what Hook would consider a busy day. I hit the intercom button. "Robert, a man named Dudek will arrive soon. You will immediately recognize him because he has a stainless-steel hook in place of his right hand. The moment he arrives, let me know."

"Has this man previously visited your office?"

"He has. Why do you ask?"

"Because you lied to me. Remember? The first time I entered your office and used your bathroom you informed me that I was the first and only disabled person to use that bathroom. That was the reason you gave me as to why your toilet facility had not been upgraded to ADA standards."

My God, this man was a pain in the ass. "Robert, that misinformation on my part was not intentional. My good man, I have not seen Mr. Dudek for a few years, and when he was here, to the best of my knowledge, he never availed himself of the toilet facilities."

There was an extended pause before Robert responded. "Pinky, when Mr. Dudek arrives, I will question him to determine if what you just told me is true."

At that moment, Robert's impertinence had vexed me to the point that I was ready to call Louis Loomer and demand he replace the miscreant, but then reality set in. I needed someone with Robert's ability to cover for me, as I might be going out of town to find a buyer for the book. Now was not the moment to seek a replacement.

"Robert, once he arrives, you can ask Mr. Dudek all the questions you feel are necessary to satisfy your concerns, and then send him into my office."

Chapter Sixteen

Bear Zabarte—Nuremberg, Germany

The kid cop drove us to the bookstore and the joint still had some of that yellow police tape hanging on the front door.

I glanced around the street. "Jesus, Juri, this neighborhood looks pretty crappy to me."

"Excuse me?"

Flo said, "Juri, I think what Bear means is the storefronts on on this block are very, very old."

Juri glanced around like he had never noticed that before. Kinda like that story Flo once told me where fish don't know they're swimming in water 'cause they're swimming in water.

Juri nodded. "Bear, you are correct. The shops on both sides of the bookstore do look old, but looks can be deceiving. The majority of Nuremberg was totally destroyed by bombing raids during the war. After the Nazis surrendered, the city fathers decided to replicate the historical old town. By the 1960's most of the reconstruction work had been completed. So these shops are not much older than my Chef, Detective Bauman."

I said, "Hey, I thought Bauman was a police detective, not a dude who cooks fancy food for fancy restaurants."

Flo said, "Bear, Chef in German means boss."

"Oh, I thought he was taking a shot at his boss."

I figured this was a good place to start getting under Juri's skin. "Kid, dissing your boss like that takes a pair of cojones the size of basketballs. Dude, you, me and Flo are a lot alike. Our bosses giant pains in the ass. Ours always sends us off on a wild goose chase that we're pretty sure is a waste of our time and his money."

I spotted a little jump in the left corner of Juri's mouth as he pulled the tape from the entrance to the bookshop and I knew the dude was going to be spilling his guts real soon.

Juri said, "Bear, Flo, I will now take you to where we found the body and be available for any questions."

Me and Flo walked into the bookshop. Even with the lights on, the joint was kinda dark and there was a weird, musty, old paper stink in the air. I've never been much of a reader so staring at shelves filled with thousands of old books didn't do much for me.

125

But I could see that Flo was getting excited, like she was a kid in a candy store.

We both trailed behind Juri until he reached a counter with a cash register. He stopped and pointed at the floor behind the counter. "This is where Herr Kaufmann was found. You can still see the faint chalk marks that show the outline of his body."

I knew me and Flo were just screwing around until Juri decided to cough up his thoughts on the investigation so far. I got down on my hands and knees so he'd think I was looking for some shit the German cops missed. After a couple of seconds, Flo said, "Juri, your Chef told our boss, Pinky, that the motive for the killing was a rare book. Do you think that's correct?"

"Ya."

She continued, "Do you know what book your Chef was talking about?"

"Ya. A first edition of Martin Luther's Achtliederbuch."

"Juri, I'm not a rare book collector. Why would Martin Luther's book be so valuable?" The way my Babe asked that question told me that she knew the answer, but she needed to find out if Juri trusted her.

"Flo, I have heard that some say the Achtliederbuch is the most valuable first edition in the world."

While Flo had the dude talking I kept pretending to look for clues on the floor like I wasn't listening.

"And I assume your team searched the store for the book?"

"We did and found nothing."

Flo said, "Juri, let's say hypothetically for a moment, if the book was found and was valuable as you said, who might want to buy it?"

Juri flashed a smile at Flo. Not just a little one, but a big fat, thank-God-somebody-finally-understands-me grin. "That was the precise question I hoped you would ask."

My knees were starting to send shooting pains to my brain so I stood up, but Juri kept on spilling his guts like I wasn't even there.

"My sources informed me that a local neo-Nazi cell decided they had to get the Achtliederbuch by whatever means necessary."

Neo-Nazis? This dude's nuttier than a fruit cake.

Flo said, "And what did they plan to do with the book?"

"They would use the proceeds from the sale for two purposes. First, to reimpose Aryan supremacy."

I said, "Juri, are you talking about the same Nazi dudes that got the crap kicked out of them in World War II?"

"No Bear, they are not the same Nazis, but the neo-Nazis of today have similar ideas. They plan to build a Pan-Aryan country within Germany's pre-war boundaries."

"I said, "Babe, help me out here. What the hell does neo mean?"

"New, or a revived form. So the neo-Nazis are a modern-day bunch of bad guys with the same old line of exterminating anyone who's not white."

I thought Juri's new-Nazi line of crap was so crazy that I didn't know what to say next, and let me tell you, that doesn't happen to me very often. I had to come up with a way to find out if Flo, who's a hell of a lot smarter than me, was buying what he was selling.

"Juri, does this joint have a throne room?"

He said, "A throne room? I do not understand what you mean by throne room."

"He means a bathroom."

I grabbed her hand, "Right, Babe, and I gotta go real bad. Let's go and see if we can find me one?"

Before she could say no, I pulled her past a line of shelves to the back of the store. Then we ducked behind a wall of old books. When I was pretty sure that Juri couldn't see or hear us, I whispered, "Babe, Pinky sent us here to set up a patsy for the cops like we've done before. I've got a funny feeling that Juri's new-Nazis could be the patsies we're looking for."

Flo whispered back, "I agree, but it almost seems too easy. However, if a bunch of neo-Nazi punks end up being our patsy, I guess it's okay with me if our job turns out to be easy this time."

"Yah, but how do we know Juri didn't just make up this new-Nazi story? Are we being fed a line of bullshit? Hell, I've never even heard of those new-Nazis and I watch TV a lot."

Flo whispered, "I've heard about them, and here's everything I know. Before we left home, I read an article that stated there were fifty-nine known neo-Nazi organizations in the Americas. There are neo-Nazi cells all over the world including Europe, Russia, and even that lovely little paradise, New Zealand."

"Come on, Babe, do we really have a bunch of new-Nazis in America?"

"I'm afraid we do. Since the war, Nazi sympathizers have kept the white supremacist concept alive. For example, take the bombing in Oklahoma City by Timothy McVeigh that killed 168 people."

"I remember that, but wasn't that McVeigh dude a few slices short of a loaf."

"He was, but he was also a right-wing terrorist who murdered 168 innocent people."

"And the American right-wing terrorists are the same sort of dudes that Juri calls the new-Nazis?"

"You've got it."

"Damn!"

"Damn is right. But the problem is worldwide. Just last summer there was a march in Berlin where a mob of far-right protesters tried to force their way into the building that houses Germany's Parliament. A recent report commissioned by the German Foreign Ministry concluded that many far-right extremist movements had emerged over the last ten years. And it's not just a German or American problem. Anders Breivik killed 77 people in Norway in 2011. And there's Brenton Harrison Tarrant, who in 2019 murdered more than 50 Muslims in Christchurch, New Zealand. And how about the mass shooting at a Pittsburgh synagogue, or—"

"You can stop there. I get the picture. Okay, we agree the new-Nazis exist and they want to get their hands on the book. All we have to do is set a trap. Get Juri to spread the word that we have the book, and those new-Nazis will come to us."

Flo shook her head. "But that won't work because Pinky has the book in Carson City."

"Damn, that's right. While we were driving Helmut to Pacific Grove he told us he gave the book to Pinky. Now what the hell are we going to do?"

She glanced at her watch. "It's close to three in the afternoon here so that means it's five in the morning back home."

"What the hell has that got to do with anything?"

"I'll call Pinky as soon as we get back to the hotel. The last time I talked to him he was thinking about finding a buyer. If he sells that book we'll lose the bait for our rattrap."

About then we heard Juri yell, "Bear, Flo, are you okay?"

Flo called, "Just fine. We're on our way back."

As we headed back to Juri, Flo whispered, "Just follow my lead."

"Gotcha, Babe."

Once we got to Juri, I said, "Couldn't find a can, but that's okay 'cause I can hold it."

Flo said, "Okay, Juri, let's say for the moment that we agree with your theory that a local group of neo-Nazis are the prime suspects for the Kaufmann murder. And let's say their motive is to obtain the Achtliederbuch. But what Bear and I don't understand is why are you so sure that any country in the world would let those neo-Nazis establish a new Aryan state."

131

Juri said, "That part is easy, Flo. Their plan is to use the money from the sale of the book to build a nuclear arsenal. The threat of a nuclear attack will force nations to accept their demands."

This guy was really beginning to scare me. I said, "Juri, let me get this straight. If those bad dudes ever got their hands on that old book they'd sell it and then build atomic bombs?"

"That's what I've been told from my sources."

Flo said, "Okay Juri, it's time we stop beating around the bush and start trusting each other."

I wasn't a hundred percent sure I trusted the young cop, at least not as much as Flo did. I grabbed her hand and said,."Sorry Juri, but I can't hold it any longer. Flo, you've got to help me find a can before I piss my pants."

Flo flashed me her 'you've got to be kidding me' glare, but before she could say anything, I pulled her away from Juri.

Once Juri was too far away to hear me, I said, "Babe, we need to talk before we say any more to that German fuzz. I know you think he's a good guy, but I'm not sure we should spill our guts until we know we can trust him."

"Okay, what's bugging you?"

I said, "I don't how to tell him that Pinky's got the book in America!"

Flo nodded, "And we need the Achtliederbuch in Nuremberg."

"I know that, but what I can't figure out is how do we get Pinky to bring the damn book here?"

Flo shook her head. "On that point, we both agree."

"Babe, I hope I'm wrong about this, but knowing how Pinky loves money, he'll never give up that book, not even to protect Helmut from a bum rap. We're wasting our time with Juri."

I glanced down the aisle at Juri, who was waiting like my faithful dog for me to finish doing a number one in the john.

Flo nodded. "I agree with you concerning Pinky so you think we have to come up with plan B."

"Huh?"

"A different plan."

"How 'bout this one Babe, Pinky's probably looking for a dude to buy the book. How about we tell him we found him a buyer in Nuremberg."

Flo thought for a second, then she shrugged her shoulders, like she wasn't sure. "I don't know. Don't forget the Nazis already murdered one man to get ahold of that book. Why should they buy the book when they can kill Pinky and take it."

"I know that, Babe, but Pinky doesn't. And me and Juri will be with him all the way. It'll be our job to make sure the boss doesn't get offed."

Juri called, "Did Bear find a bathroom?"

Flo said, "Yes he did, and he'll be out in a second."

Then she looked at me and giggled. "Bear, our situation reminds me of that musical we saw in Reno, _The Man of La Mancha_. Do you remember?"

"Yup, I sure do. The one about that old Spanish dude, Donkey Hotee, and his buddy, Sancho Something."

Flo nodded. I think she was happy 'cause I remembered that stupid show 'bout an old dude riding around Spain on a horse trying to knock over windmills with a long stick.

She said, "Do you recall the part when Don Quixote got himself into a really bad situation, like the pickle we're in now? His old sidekick, Sancho Panza, told him, 'Whether the pitcher hits the stone, or the stone hits the pitcher, it's not going to be good for the pitcher.' Bear, from this moment on we have to remember that the neo-Nazis are the stones and we, including Pinky, are the pitchers."

I said, "Got it! If we're not real careful it's not going to be good for us pitchers. Babe, are we going to tell Juri that we've got a plan to get the book to Germany?"

"Not yet. Let's see what he wants to do for the rest of the day."

Chapter Seventeen

Pinky Delmont—Carson City, Nevada

My day in court had disintegrated into a total farce due to a legal blunder by one of Willow's less talented underlings. As I pondered if I should summon up the strength to contact my ex-wife and register a complaint, Robert's booming voice came over the intercom and interrupted my thought process.

"Pinky, Mr. Dudek he is standing by my desk and he wants to see you at once. I informed him that according to your standard office policy, he would need to make an appointment."

"Robert, during my phone call with Mr. Dudek I asked him to come to my office so he has a de-facto appointment. And, in the future, Mr. Dudek, and only Mr. Dudek, is exempt from my appointment policy. Send him in at once and do not disturb us for any reason."

"I will do that. By the way, according to Mr. Dudek, he has never used your office toilet facility."

The door opened and Hook marched in with a confident air, as if he were a pirate seeking a site to bury his booty.

"Shyster, how about pouring me four fingers of your excellent Scotch whiskey."

The thought of an extremely large payday lifted my sagging spirits. I spun my chair around, pulled out two glasses and poured a generous portion into each receptacle.

Hook smiled. "Okay, what's your story?"

I tipped my glass in Hook's direction and said, "My good man, I seek a buyer for a rare book I have in my possession. However, as this book is—"

"Save your breath. You're talking about a private sale, correct?"

Before I could respond, Hook tossed the golden nectar into his mouth and swallowed as if he had been desiccated by an unrelenting desert sun. I was shocked to note that the cretin had not given his tastebuds the opportunity to savor the complex nuances that graced the glorious elixir. Hook slammed his empty glass on my desk in a gesture that demanded I pour him a refill. As the whiskey cascaded into his glass, I made a mental note to stock an inferior Scotch in my credenza as the man's palette seemed incapable of determining an outstanding spirit from common swill.

"If it's a private sale, all you have to do is get the book to Las Vegas." After he tossed down the second shot, Hook continued, "Of course, I'll have to go with the book to Vegas 'cause my contact only deals with me."

I said, "So you are not at liberty to provide me with the name of the buyer?"

Hook held the pointed end of his hook a quarter inch above my desk and glared at me, as if challenging my right to ask that question. "Shyster, even if I wanted to, and I don't, my contact, and only my contact, knows the name of the buyer. By the way, for my services I will be paid a $10,000 finders fee.

A cold chill raced down my spinal column as I recalled my last trip with Hook. Our little stopover in New Jersey turned into a helicopter ride that nearly cost me my life. Under the dark cloud of that recollection, I took a sip and let the delightful liquid linger on my tongue for a moment. Considering my last disaster with this man, plus his exorbitant finders fee, I needed time to decide if I was ready to travel to Las Vegas with him.

As I watched the honed tip of his hook hover over my beloved, hand-rubbed, mahogany desk, I realized that bringing this man into my little adventure may have been a mistake. However, as Grandfather Delmont was fond of reminding me, 'in for a penny, in for a pound'.

I had in my possession a book that could be worth millions.

I needed this man to find a buyer for the book and if that included traveling to Las Vegas, and paying him for his troubles, so be it.

However, considering our last near-fatal previous partnership, I required a little more time to determine if I had any wiggle room concerning my agreement with him. Perhaps a brief discussion with my favorite ex-wife, a brilliant attorney to see if she could provide me with some prudent advice.

"My good man, I may have some court appearances scheduled over the next few days. I have to be sure I can reschedule those before I can commit to traveling to Las Vegas." I glanced at my watch which showed it was nearly five in the afternoon. "Once we conclude this meeting, I have just enough time to contact the court clerk. I will call you first thing in the morning to let you know if I have been unable to adjust my court schedule, thus cancelling our Vegas trip."

Before I could blink, the point of his hook dropped onto my desk and he dragged it until he had created an inch-deep abyss roughly the length of two playing cards across the once pristine mahogany.

"Shyster, I'm picking up vibes that tell me you're looking for a way out. I spent years developing my contacts. Pinky, once I entered your office you were on the hook for my ten thousand dollar finder's fee even if you backed out of our deal." Then he then pulled the point and lengthened the mahogany canyon another few inches. "Come hell or high water, tomorrow morning I'm riding with you to Vegas in that fancy new car of yours."

"Hook, I hear you loud and clear. As I previously stated, I have to check my court calendar first."

Without another word, Hook lifted his metal weapon off my desk and stormed out of my office.

After a moment, to allow time for Hook to leave the building, I hit the intercom. "Robert, check my court calendar. Am I free to take a couple of days off?"

"Yes, you are clear for three days."

"Excellent. Earlier I told you that in the future, Mr. Dudek, was exempt from making an appointment. I am now rescinding his exemption."

Robert said, "Let me be sure I have this straight. Anytime anyone walks in and asks to see you, I am to tell them you are available only with an appointment. Is that correct?"

"Correct!"

"And Mr. Dudek is now back on your do-not-disturb list."

"Again, correct."

There was a pause, and then Robert continued, "Pinky, as a paraplegic, I have learned to ignore another man's disability, but for some reason I can not take my eyes off Mr. Dudek's hook."

I glanced down at the Grand Canyon that now disfigured my beloved desk. "Robert, I agree with your most apt observation. First thing tomorrow, you are to find someone in town that can repair a deep gouge in my hand-rubbed mahogany desk."

"I'll take care of that before I do anything else. Where are you going on your short vacation?"

"Las Vegas, and it is a business trip. Only fools vacation in Vegas."

"I'll agree to that."

"And Robert, from now on, anytime Mr. Dudek enters this building unannounced, you should contact the Police Department and ask them to send someone over to pick up my contribution to their Toys for Children fund."

"Does the Police Department collect money for that all year long?"

"They do not. However, the Chief and I set up that code a few years ago just in case one of my clients became, let us say, overly agitated."

"Pinky, I'm beginning to understand your style and I like it."

"Thank you, Robert. Now, I am going home to pack, but before I leave I want to make sure you know there are three exceptions to my appointment-only policy. Bear and Flo are two, and the third is Willow Stone."

"Got it. Is that all?"

"Yes."

Before I left the office, I pulled the FedEx box that contained Martin Luther's Achtliederbuch from my safe and slipped it into my briefcase. As I drove home, I continued to remind myself that a first edition of Luther's tome could be worth millions, enough for me to retire and live the life I deserved, wherever I wanted to reside.

Back in in the safety of my home, I poured myself a glass of red wine, and considered my trip to Las Vegas with Hook and determined I had two choices.

If I sold the book to a buyer in Vegas, my legal obligation to my client, Helmut Kaufmann, would have to end due to the fact that I had stepped over a moral and ethical line.

If I stayed in Carson City, my opportunity to become a rich playboy would come to a disappointing conclusion.

During my second glass of wine, I placed a call to Willow, forgetting that she had a new number. As we had once shared a bed, and with her legal expertise, I valued her advice concerning my present dilemma.

After the third ring, I was shuffled off to her recording device where I left her a message. "Willow, I know you changed numbers, but I'm counting on you to check your old recordings. Here is the reason why I have to talk with you. This may sound strange coming from me, but I am struggling with a dilemma that some would say borders on the edge of legal ethics. Please return my call as soon as possible."

Before I could take another sip of wine my phone beeped.

I answered, trusting that Willow was on the other end, but instead I heard an unwelcome voice.

"Pinky, this is Flo."

Cutting to the chase to free up my call from Willow, I said, "Florence, have you found me a first rate suspect?"

"Not only first rate, but a prime suspect."

My ears perked up. Perhaps this woman had already solved my quandary. I asked, "According to whom?"

"According to Juri Vogel, a member of the Kriminalpolizei section of the Bavarian State Police. The very cop assigned by your buddy,

Detective Joseph Bauman, to keep an eye on us while we snooped around Nuremberg."

Could it be that all my problems were beginning to fall into place?

"Florence, under those circumstances you and Bear have done excellent work. Has the suspect been arrested?"

"Not yet. That's why I called."

My euphoria vanished. "Not under arrest? Explain why."

Florence informed me that the prime suspect was not a man, but a local group of neo-Nazis.

"My good woman, if the case against the neo-Nazis is so obvious, why has Detective Bauman's underling, Juri Vogel, not made an arrest?"

Florence's voice rose, as if on the edge of anger. "Because Juri's sure the neo-Nazis strangled Konrad Kaufmann for the first edition of Martin Luther's Achtliederbuch! The same book you had in your office while we drove Helmut to your Pacific Grove condo!"

"Florence, calm down. I have had a particularly stressful day. Now, we both know I possess the book. But you still have not answered my query as to what the book has to do with arresting a gang of killers in Nuremberg?"

"Vogel's informant told him they strangled Helmut's uncle for that book, damn it! Vogel's positive that if the book was here, in Nuremberg, he could use it to flush out the neo-Nazis."

I sat down and pondered my situation. "Florence, if I overnighted the book to Detective Bauman, would he agree to immediately drop all charges against my client, Helmut Kaufmann?"

Florence said, "I can't guarantee that because presently there's a disagreement between Vogel and his boss, Bauman, concerning who is the prime suspect, your client Helmut, or the neo-Nazis."

"Obviously, their disagreement greatly concerns me. Even if Vogel is correct, what would eventually happen to my book?"

"I would assume that once the neo-Nazis were arrested, you would get the book back."

"My dear, when you assume something, you make an ass out of both you and me. I made a promise to my grandfather to never assume anything. Are you telling me that if I give up my book there is a possibility that my priceless first edition, potentially worth millions, might never be returned to me?"

She said, "Let me get this straight. Are you telling me that you're not willing to send that fake copy of the Achtliederbuch to Nuremberg to save Helmut from a phony charge of murder?"

"Florence, my final decision is not as straightforward as you suggest. I do have a responsibility to my client, but not to the detriment of my personal health and welfare."

"Your health and welfare?" Florence yelled. "What does selling your client down the river have to do with that?"

"As I am sure you are aware, I am the sole proprietor of my practice. As such, all my benefits: health insurance and retirement, are my responsibility. The Achtliederbuch is my guarantee that all those obligations concerning my well-being would be covered."

"That's the biggest line of bull you have ever tried to feed me. Pinky, if you do not ship that damn book to us in the next twenty-four hours, once we return to Carson City, I will file misfeasance charges with the Nevada Bar Association to make sure that you are disbarred!"

My phone beeped, indicating I had another call. "Florence, I have to hang up. I will contact you within the next twenty-four hours with my decision."

I hit the button. "Hello?"

"Pinky, it's Willow. You didn't sound like yourself when you left your message, sort of unsettled and that's not like you. Are you okay?"

The warm tone of Willow's voice pulled me back from Florence's ridiculous threat.

"My love, I want to pose a hypothetical question to you. Let us say there is an attorney who has a client that owns a valuable book, and the client is completely unaware concerning the value of that book. To further muddy the waters, that same client gave the book to his attorney to cover a portion of his retainer. Today, that hypothetical attorney is looking into the possibility of selling the book."

"Pinky, the fact that the hypothetical attorney accepted the book as part of his retainer informs me that he must have been aware that the book had value, otherwise he would not have accepted it as a portion of his retainer. Is that correct?"

I hesitated, but my eternal love for this woman forced me to tell the truth. "You are correct. The attorney was aware the book had potential value, and in anticipation of your next question, the hypothetical client was not aware of the book's value."

She said, "So your question is if the book is sold by the hypothetical attorney, is he ethically required to turn a percentage of the proceeds over to the hypothetical client?"

"You are correct. That is my question."

"Pinky, I find it hard to believe that this is a hypothetical situation. Am I correct that you are talking about one of your clients?"

Again I hesitated. As long as we continued this hypothetical game we avoided putting each other on the spot.

"Pinky, I'm waiting for an answer, and the longer I wait the more I'm sure that you are talking about a specific interaction with one of your clients."

I decided to go all in. "Willow, you are right. My question concerns one of my clients."

"Then I fear you are not going to like my answer. Pinky, you have not given me a question concerning ethical behavior. No, I fear you've placed your greed ahead of your client's best interests. Were you going to provide your client with the best defense, or did your concern over the value of the book cloud your legal judgement?"

"My dear, I took into consideration my building of a solid defense strategy, but I—"

"No buts, Pinky. I guessed from the beginning of our conversation that you were not posing a hypothetical situation. You have an actual client who owned a valuable book. You now have that book and are considering selling it. The answer from your ex-wife, who happens to be an attorney with ethics, is that you cannot sell the book without at least splitting the proceeds with your client. Finally, as an officer of the court, you are required to defend your client with all the resources at your disposal."

"My dear, it is possible that I did not make the situation clear."

"Pinky, your motives are very clear to me. Now, if you will excuse me, I have to finish filling the dishwasher. And as for any future relationship between us, save your energy. I hope you find happiness with someone, but that partnership will not include me. Goodbye!"

Momentarily stunned by my ex-wife's frankness, I sat down and considered what I should do next.

I could fly to Nuremberg and turn the book over to the police.

Or, I could drive to Las Vegas with Hook and reap a potential, giant payout.

Steadfast with the knowledge that I seldom make the wrong decision, I sat down at my desk and typed an email to Florence:

Florence,
In my opinion, a truly efficient German law enforcement organization would be able to build a murder case against a local individual, or group, without my book to 'flush them out' as you stated during our phone conversation today. Therefore, I will leave around 1:00 am

and drive to Las Vegas with Hook who claims he has found a buyer for my book. The drive and meeting will take us approximately eight hours, allowing plenty of time to FedEx the book to you if, for any reason, the potential sale falls through.

J. Pincus Delmont

Next I called my office.

"Law Office of J. Pincus Delmont. Presently the office is closed. After the beep, please leave a message and someone will get back during regular business hours."

After the tone I said, "Robert, just a call to remind you of my trip tomorrow to Las Vegas with Mr. Dudek. Should the need arise, you can reach me on my mobile any time. Goodbye."

Finally, I called Hook.

"Hello."

I glanced at my watch. It was six-thirty.

"Hook, this is Pinky. At midnight I will pick you up at my office parking lot for the drive to Las Vegas."

"Hey, I thought we're going to leave in the morning. What the hell is going on? I'm not even packed yet."

"My good man, as my court schedule is extremely tight there is no reason to pack. Our round trip will take us no more than twenty-four hours. Now I'm going to take a short nap, and as we will be driving to Vegas through the night. I suggest you do the same."

Chapter Eighteen

Bear Zabarte—Nuremberg, Germany

I should have known better than to fall for Flo's rocks hitting plates bullshit. Damn, if we'd told Juri we knew the book was sitting in America, we wouldn't have had to spend the rest of the day picking up and checking out about fifty-million books that were sitting on shelves, stacked on the floor, and stuffed into boxes in the backroom. And before you start wanting to burn my ass, I know that Flo would get all over me for exaggerating how many books we looked at but trust me, after spending all day of looking for something I knew wasn't there, it seemed like it had to be at least fifty million.

I glanced at my watch. It showed 1:15. Thats' it! I couldn't take this bullshit any longer. I yelled, "Okay, Juri, I think we're done here. How 'bout we get out of this joint and grab a beer?"

Juri said, "I agree it is a perfect time for a beer but I have work to finish back in my office. But just incase you and Flo go, I need to teach you how to order a beer in German."

Flo snickered, "Knowing my man, that's a lesson he's been waiting for. If fact, I'm not sure why it took you so long."

Juri stared at Flo like he didn't get the joke. Then, sort of like a light bulb turned on, the dude flashed a little grin at Flo. From that smile on, Juri loosened up a whole bunch.

"Flo, Bear, I'm beginning to understand how American humor works. Okay, Bear, when you walk into any bar in Germany, all you have to say is ein bier, bitte."

"Juri, let me be sure I got this. So ein is one. Bier is beer. And bitte is please. Right?"

He nodded.

I said, "So let's say after four or five beers, I've got to take a piss. How do I say that in German?"

"Wo ist die toilette?

"So Wo is where. And ist is is. De is the. And toilet is the john. Right?"

Juri nodded. "Ja."

"And that's yes! Babe, you never told me that learning how to talk German was this easy."

Juri glanced at his watch. "I could skip my office work and take you to see some World War Two Nazi buildings. Tomorrow we will begin looking for the new Nazis, as you like to call them."

Flo frowned, like somebody just stepped on her little toe. "Juri, how long will this trip to see the old Nazi buildings take?"

"A couple of hours, perhaps three."

"I know it's still early but I'm pooped out. Probably just jet lag. Could we do the tour tomorrow and then let Bear order in German for the first time?"

"Of course."

As he dropped us off at the hotel, Juri said, "Have a good rest. I'll pick you up tomorrow morning around ten. Okay?"

I saw Flo flash Juri her 'I'm all pooped out' look, but I didn't fall for that jet lag crap 'cause I know she's tougher then a concrete fence post.

She waved to Juri, and said, "See you tomorrow."

As soon as Juri walked out of the door, she bounced across the lobby and I could see that I was right, she wasn't pooped out, she was ready for something.

We hopped into the elevator and rode up to the fifth floor. Once our room door closed, Flo ran over to her laptop, read something, and shook her head like she was pissed off.

She asked, "What time is it?"

I glanced at my watch. A little after one-thirty. Why?"

"We have to call Pinky."

I walked over to one of those great little refrigerators they have in fancy hotel rooms, pulled out a beer, popped the cap, took a big swig, and said, "Babe, okay, but what's the time got to do with calling the boss?"

"Because I just read the email he sent me on my laptop."

"Babe, he's there and we're here. What did he say that's got your skivvies all twisted up?"

"Hook has lined up a buyer for the book in Vegas."

I almost said what book, but then I remembered that Flo was probably talking about the Acktersomething, the book the new-Nazis were looking for when they offed Helmut's uncle. I took another long swig before I said, "So what does Pinky doing something stupid like going to Vegas have to do with us? And you still didn't tell me why you asked what time it was?"

She stormed over and grabbed the beer out of my hand.

"Bear, there are times when you seem to be mentally out-to-lunch. It's as if your thought processes exist in another dimension. Now, to answer your first question: If Pinky drives to Vegas and sells the book, what's Juri going to use to flush the neo-Nazis out of their hiding place? Second, why did I ask you the time of day? Don't you recall that when we landed in

Nuremberg I told you to reset your watch ahead nine hours?"

"Yup."

"Do you know why you needed to reset your watch?"

"Nope."

My babe's face started to get that scrunched up look she gets when she's really pissed off at me. "Because there's a nine-hour time difference between Nuremberg and Carson City, that's why!"

That's when Mr. Johnson's high school class popped into my head. When I was in my senior year at Elko High my geography teacher had this really cool globe with dark lines that went from the north pole at the top to the south pole at the bottom. He told us the dark lines were time zone lines and he showed us where Elko High School was on the globe, in the Pacific time zone, and then he found New York City, in the Eastern time zone, like three lines away. Then he told us that when you went toward the east and crossed a time zone line, you had to move your watch a whole hour ahead. Like when it was nine o'clock in the morning in Elko, it'd be lunch time in New York. Now I know Flo thinks I'm pretty dumb at times, but I was damn sure that Nuremberg was a bunch of lines east of New York. So now I knew why Flo told me to move my watch ahead nine hours. My babe hit a home run on that one.

"I've got it, Babe. If it's 1:30 in the afternoon here, it's about 4:30 in the morning in Carson City. Right?"

Her face lost that scrunched up look and got all smiley. "Right."

"So what's the time in Carson City got to do with that beer you won't let me drink?"

She looked at the bottle like she forgot that she was holding it and then she handed it back to me.

"Sorry, Bear. I guess I didn't want to wakeup Pinky so early the morning."

"But I thought his email said Hook and Pinky were driving to Vegas?"

"That's right. I'll bet he's driving rather than flying because he wants to show off that new car of his to Hook." She got that nasty grin on her puss. "How about I call him now and find out?"

My babe found him in her contacts, tapped in the phone number, and hit the speaker button. After the fourth ring we heard, "Pinky here. Is this Florence?"

I said, "And Bear. Boss, how's driving that fancy car to Vegas working out?"

"Excellent. Presently, I am nearing the end of the first leg of the excursion."

I said, "And Hook's with you?"

"He is."

"Hi, Hook. How's it hanging?"

A muffled voice said, "Just fine. And you?"

"I'm good. Boss, why didn't you and Hook just fly to Vegas?"

Pinky said, "Where I go and how I get there are my business. Did you and Florence have something important to talk about, or are you just testing the capability of the world-wide cell phone network?"

I said, "Boss, we need that damn book!"

"I have already provided Florence with my timeline for the book. When I reach Tonopah, I will recharge my Mercedes ESQ and get some breakfast. In another four hours I will arrive in Las Vegas. I should have a final answer concerning the book within six hours."

Flo edged me aside with her elbow. "Pinky, don't forget what I said about my visit to the Bar Association."

"Florence, you will receive my response, via email, within six hours. Goodbye!"

After Pinky hung up, I said, "Babe, what was your visit to the Bar Association crap all about?"

"If he sells that book, your buddy Helmut's goose is cooked! I told Pinky if he sold the book, I'd go to the Bar Association and get him disbarred."

Flo knows a lot more about everything then I do, but maybe she didn't think of what could happen to me and her if Pinky can't be a lawyer anymore.

"But then the boss won't be a lawyer then me and you will lose our golden ticket. Babe, from the first time you met Pinky you held his ass to the fire. Like how you did such a great job getting him to pay us more money than we're worth. And a few years ago when you conned him into giving us health insurance. And a couple of years ago you made him add dental insurance. And last year you got him to give us some weird thing that will pay us when we get old."

"That weird thing's called a 401 (k) plan. And Pinky doesn't pay for everything on our 401 (k) plan. We put in money each month and he matches that with the same amount."

"Babe, what I'm trying to say that we'll lose all that good stuff if Pinky's not a lawyer."

Flo sighed, "I agree. Working for Pinky has placed us on the horns of a dilemma."

"Huh?"

"Bear, the horns of a dilemma is an idiom that refers to a situation where you are confronted with making a decision based on two options, and no matter which option you choose, you'll get hurt."

"So you're saying that me and you are screwed no matter what we do?"

"Not totally. If Pinky sells that book all we lose is money and benefits. It's Helmut that's really screwed. He'll spend the rest of his life in a German prison."

"That's more of a bummer than losing some bucks and stuff."

Flo took my hand, the one without a bottle of beer, and said, "At least we'll still have each other."

I drained the beer and grabbed a second. "Right, Babe. And I can always go back to tending bar at The Old Globe. Our life won't be so bad." But I knew I was just blowing smoke. There's no way a babe as good lookin' as Flo would stick with a looser who's gonna spend the rest of his life behind the bar at Carson City's crappiest dive bar.

Chapter Nineteen

Pinky Delmont—Las Vegas, Nevada

Hook met me in my office parking lot at midnight and inside four hours we were on the outskirts of Tonopah.

Thankfully, Hook fell asleep almost as soon as we cleared the city limits of Carson City so my drive through the first half of the journey was peaceful.

Suddenly an animal darted across the highway and I had to jerk the wheel to avoid the creature. That unexpected movement caused my passenger to wake.

He yawned and glanced out the window at the dark Nevada wasteland. "Pinky, you're a pain in the ass, but this is without a doubt the coolest car I've ever sat in."

"Thank you. I have to admit that this will be the longest drive I have made with my new car. As you know, it is a battery-powered vehicle. I have a touch of range anxiety for the first leg of our journey."

"Jesus, I didn't even notice this was an electric car. How far can it go?"

I exhibited a touch more confidence than I actually felt due to the fact that the published range of my Mercedes ESQ was approximately 300 miles. However, the salesman told me that if I kept my speed at a steady 60 mph, the vehicle should be capable of reaching close to 400 miles. "It is possible we could drive all the way to Vegas without recharging. However, if we run out of battery power, we could end up stuck in the middle Nevada. So, I am going to break our trip in half. The first leg of our journey will be approximately 220 miles. We'll stop in Tonopah for breakfast while my Mercedes charges."

"I don't know nothing about these new electric cars."

"My model, the EQS 580 4Matic has an electric motor on each axle. Mercedes estimates this all-wheel-drive model can go from zero to 60 mph in just a hair over four seconds."

"Jesus."

"Once we reach Tonopah, the vehicle can recharge 70 percent of its battery in about 35 minutes using a fast charger."

Hook frowned, "That's about the same as it'll take us to eat breakfast. But what happens if you're wrong. What the hell happens if we run out of battery power before we reach Tonopah?"

In a casual manner that belied my true feelings, I replied, "I will call AAA and request a tow to the nearest charging station. Relax, Hook, and enjoy riding in a vehicle that set me back more than a hundred thousand dollars."

"Jesus, more than a hundred big ones!"

Eventually, Hook sat back and stared out the window while I turned on my classical music playlist and listened to Chopin, Bach, and Beethoven through the outstanding, upgraded sound system I had purchased when I bought my Mercedes.

When my car eased into Tonopah, the dash indicator showed I still had 130 miles left on the batteries so the aforementioned range of more than 300 miles was proven to be correct. So much for range anxiety! The large screen on the dashboard area directed me to the nearest fast-charging station. Conveniently, the charging station was located next to a restaurant that advertised they served breakfast twenty-fours a day. It look as if man and vehicle would get recharged for the last leg of the drive.

Despite our midnight departure, I was as bright as a button as I looked over the menu. Usually, I consumed a light breakfast consisting of juice, toast, and coffee. But during the stop in Tonopah, I ordered the Silver

Miner's special and ingested enough calories to complete the remaining drive to Las Vegas.

Ten minutes into the final leg to Vegas, Hook fell asleep again. Some hours later, as we approached Sin City, the traffic increased with the morning rush and I shook Hooks' shoulder to wake him. Just before we reached the famous Vegas Strip, I said, "Hook, where do we go from here?"

He was still groggy when he mumbled a few left and right turns, which made no sense to me.

I snapped, "Damn it! Wake up and give me those directions again."

He sat up and shook the cobwebs from his brain. "Turn left at the next signal. Then turn right at the first street and grab a right into the parking lot at Smith's Hardware."

I followed his instructions to the letter and drove into the parking lot of Smith's Hardware store.

As there were no cars parked in the lot, I drove up to the entrance and Hook peered out the side window. He said, "We're too early. They don't open for an hour. We passed a Denny's a half a block back and I could use a cup of coffee."

"I agree."

I retraced our route to the Denny's and drove around the parking lot until I found five empty parking spaces near the back of the building. I pulled into the middle slot at an angle so no one would be able to park in any of the five spots.

"Shyster, you coulda' parked straighter, and a hell of a lot closer to the front door."

"I know that. This way I will protect my new vehicle from the wanton dents caused by all the cretins who drive old VWs or Datsuns. We can also use the distance to the front entrance to stretch our legs. God knows I could use a little walk."

We entered the restaurant, found a booth and ordered coffee.

"Hook, it's time we talk about the pending sale. What is our next step?"

He pulled a paper out of his pocket and said, "Okay, we go back to that hardware store and find the small engine repair section. The man behind the counter will take us to a back room. Then the buyer will enter. You will give him the book and he will take the book to his appraiser while we wait. If the book is legit, or you might say, authentic, he will make you an offer."

"Hold on. You never told me that I had to hand my valuable book over to a complete stranger and let him leave the room with it!"

Hook glanced over his shoulder, as if there might be someone watching and listening to us.

"Hey, you think too much like your shyster buddies. The dude I'm working with has standards in contrast to all you legal dudes. Pinky, think about it. If the guy stiffs you, he'll never get anyone to trust him again. And that goes for you too. God help you if you've put lipstick on a pig and try to sell him a phony book." Hook glanced at his cup. "See if you can catch the waitress' eye. I need a refill."

A very uncomfortable feeling was beginning to creep into my bones. What do I do if the buyer vanishes with my priceless asset. And what happens to me if the buyer decides my book is a worthless copy?

"Hook, what if I feel his offer is too low?"

"That's up to you. But whatever you do, you'll still owe me my finder's fee of ten thousand clams."

The precarious nature of my situation began to scare me. In my opinion, the book was completely authentic. But I was a lawyer, not someone who appraised old books. There was no way that I should be held responsible for my error concerning the books authenticity.

However, as I glanced at the shiny tip on Hook's right arm, I realized that this trip to Las Vegas might be no different than our journey to New Jersey. Had this man placed me into another life-threatening situation? Instead of the Atlantic Ocean, would the Las

Vegas mob dump me into the five-hundred-foot deep, icy-cold water of Lake Mead?

I had always known that Hook lived on the edge of the dark side, but just now I realized that every time I had associated with him, I placed my life at risk.

As the waitress refilled both of our cups, I decided that I was not ready to turn my life over to someone else, so I said, "Please excuse me. I need to use the restroom."

Hook did not even look up from his cup as I slipped out the front door of the coffee shop and ran to my car. As I pulled out of the parking lot I checked the rearview mirror and Hook was nowhere in sight.

Now alone, I asked my iPhone assistant, "Siri, route me to the airport."

She responded, "McCarran International?"

"Correct."

In her clipped British accent, Siri directed me the two miles to the airport.

A half-block outside the airport entrance, I spotted an off-site parking garage that advertised sheltered parking. Just what I needed for my new Mercedes. I pulled in and a young man approached my vehicle.

He said, "Wow, I've never seen one of these before. Are you going to leave your car with us?"

"As this Mercedes ESQ is the first model the company has shipped west of the Mississippi, I will leave it once you promise me that my vehicle will be sheltered at all times. And you will charge the vehicle. And that you are capable of getting me to the departure area of the airport within the next ten minutes."

He pulled a walkie talkie out of his back pocket and said, "We need the shuttle at the front gate. Pronto!"

He handed me a clipboard that contained a standard parking contract. By the time I had filled in the blanks and signed the contract, the shuttle was waiting for me. I grabbed my briefcase and jumped in.

The shuttle driver said, "What airline?"

"I don't know yet. I will let you know."

Trusting that Robert would have arrived at his desk, I pulled my cell out and said, "Hey, Siri, call my office."

Halfway through the first ring, Robert answered, "Law Office of J. Pincus Delmont, Robert V. Silva speaking. How may I help you?"

"Robert, this is Pinky. I do not have time for any idle chit-chat, so just do as I tell you. I need a reservation on a non-stop round trip flight from McCarran International to Nuremberg, Germany. Book me in first class."

I heard Robert's fingers hit his keyboard. Then he responded, "Sorry, Pinky, there are no non-stops flights from McCarran International to Nuremberg, Germany."

I sighed. A layover at any airport was a monumental waste of my time and in my profession, time is money. "Fine. Do what you must."

"Okay. I've found a flight but there is one problem. First class is sold out. They do have one business class seat left. Do you want me to reserve that?"

I pondered for a moment. During my entire legal career I had never flown anywhere in anything less than first class and—

"Pinky, I'm sorry, but I need your answer now. The flight takes off in a little more than an hour from now and I don't know where you are calling me from. Are you close enough to reach the boarding gate before it is closed?"

"Book the business class."

"Got it. Okay, you will be spending two hours and nineteen minutes in the Minneapolis-Saint Paul Airport, and eight hours and forty-five minutes in the Amsterdam Airport. You'll arrive at Nuremberg, at six-twenty tomorrow evening. I'll send the information along with your boarding pass to your email and . . . hold on, you'll need your passport to board the plane."

"Robert, you do not work for a fool. I always carry my passport in my briefcase. But that reminds me, I believe in the Rolodex, under TSA, Lu kept my TSA—Known Traveler Number."

"One moment. I've got it. I'll add that number to your reservation so you can bypass the long TSA line."

"Good. Now, to my next point. From this day forward, Hook Dudek will be considered persona non grata to me and my legal practice. As such, I will not talk with him should he call, nor will he be welcome to enter my office. If by any chance, Hook does attempt to contact me while I am gone, inform him that I have received an emergency phone call from a client in Nuremberg and I had to catch an immediate flight to Germany. Please cut a $15,000 check for Mr. Dudeck to pay him for his efforts. That should calm him down, but if not, inform him that upon my return I will seek a permanent injunction against him for stalking. And I am positive a judge will further agree that Mr. Dudek will not be allowed to come closer than 250 yards of me, my car, my home, or my office."

"Got it. Pinky, I just sent the boarding pass to your email. Bon Voyage!"

"Thank you, Robert. I will return to my office in a few days. Oh, I almost forgot. Send an email to Florence informing her of the airline I am booked on, the flight number, and the arrival time at the Nuremberg airport, so she can arrange to pick me up once my plane has landed, and tell her I have the book with me. Again, thank you, Robert."

As the shuttle reached the departure area. The driver said, "Hey, you know what airline yet?"

I glanced at the email on my cell phone. "Yes, it is Delta."

"That's about a hundred feet ahead!"

As I departed the shuttle, I smiled to myself, confident with the knowledge that I was doing everything I could to fulfill my moral, ethical, and legal responsibilities required to serve my client, Helmut Kaufmann.

Chapter Twenty

Bear Zabarte—Nuremberg, Germany

Sometime that night, I woke up when Flo's computer dinged like it does when she gets an email. My Babe? She sleeps like a rock and doesn't hear anything short of a freight train running through the bedroom. As I drifted off, I told my brain to remind Flo to turn off her computer while we were sleeping. The next morning, I was still sawing logs when Flo shook me.

"Bear, wake up. Pinky's on his way to Nuremberg."

The minute, 'Pinky's on his way to Nuremberg', filtered through my thick skull, I rolled out of the sack.

"Babe, I guess we get to keep our jobs. Do we have time this morning to fool around?"

"I've already showered, so not this morning. Get up and while you get dressed I'll read you Pinky's email."

I took a quick shower and while I dried off, Flo read me what Pinky's email said. It turned out that Pinky didn't send it. The email came from that hard-ass dude who took over for Lu, but Flo didn't have to tell me that 'cause I knew it wasn't Pinky's writing when the email didn't start out with his usual line of crap like how he was there to protect the innocent. Robert got right to the meat and told us the boss was on his way to Nuremberg. He was bringing the book, and we needed to pick him up at the airport around six-thirty.

"Babe, do you think we should tell Juri that Pinky's coming today with the book?"

"I don't know. Let's go eat breakfast. Maybe some coffee will help me figure out what to do next."

We went downstairs and just like the day before, the hotel laid out another great spread of food. While I chowed down on big slabs of cheese, slices of meat, and the best damn bread I'd ever eaten, Flo said, "In my opinion, we've got to trust someone in this situation and I trust Juri a lot more than his stuffy boss, Detective Bauman. What do you think?"

The bread was great and this joint had the best damn strawberry jam I'd ever seen. And trust me, I've downed a bucket full of great strawberry jam. As I spread a thick layer of jam onto a hefty slab of almost black bread, Flo planted one of her sharp elbows into my side.

"Bear, your opinion is important to me. Swallow that mouthful of bread and jam and answer me."

I gulped down the big bite. "Babe, I agree. We'll go with Juri. Somewhere between now and the time we go to the airport to pick up Pinky, we'll figure out a way to tell Juri that Pinky's bringing the book. What I haven't figured out yet is how do we tell Juri that Helmut had the book before he flew to Nuremberg."

While I downed two more slices of bread and jam, Flo left to brush her teeth. After I finished a last slab of bread and strawberry jam, I zipped upstairs, brushed my teeth, and me and Flo met Juri in the lobby around ten.

As Juri drove away from our hotel, he told us, "Okay, during the day I will give you a history lesson on why Hitler decided that Nuremberg would be his city for Nazi Party rallies. During medieval times Nuremberg was the center of the German Reichstag, which is a German word for their parliament. That is why Hitler decided Nuremberg was the perfect center for his Nazi party rallies. Also, the Nazis were a strong political force in Nuremberg. Flo, am I going too fast?"

"Not for me. How about you, Bear?"

"Except for that medieval Reich crap, I'm with you."

Juri said, "Okay, in 1933, Hitler began construction in a eleven square kilometer area in the southeastern part of Nuremberg for his party's mass meetings. Only a few components of the Rally Grounds were ever completed. Some structures never got beyond the foundations, or half-completed shells, and all construction stopped when the Second World War began in 1939. The remains of two huge structures bear witness to the megalomania of the Nazi regime."

He drove through what looked like a park and then stopped the car. We got out and he pointed through the branches of a bunch of trees and I could see a giant building.

Juri said, "Bear, that structure is the monumental Congress Hall. Hitler wanted a special building for the Party Congress with seating for at least 50,000."

"No wonder that joint looks so big."

Juri continued, "Hitler's crew started construction on the Congress Hall in 1935. It was designed to reach twenty-one stories high, but when work was suspended in September 1939 they had only reached the height of ten stories. Even at half the height, and without the planned roof, Congress Hall is an impressive structure, and today it is the largest surviving relic of Hitler's Third Reich."

Flo said, "I've been to Rome and from the outside that building reminds me of the Roman Colosseum."

"Flo, you have a good eye. During a visit to Italy, Hitler saw the colosseum and decided to use a similar concept for the Congress Hall. But he wanted his building to be twenty-one stories high, a third higher than the Roman Colosseum."

I said, "Hey, wasn't Mussolini running Italy when Hitler was around? Do you think Hitler was in a pissing match with Mussolini?"

Juri chuckled, "Bear, you might be correct. Now let us return to the car so I can show you that the Congress Hall was a harbinger of Hitler's eventual failure."

I said, "What the hell has a harbinger got to do with anything? Dude, we all know Hitler lost the war."

Flo said, "Bear, I think that Juri was trying to say that the people didn't realize this building could have predicted Hitler's eventual failure."

"Flo is correct. Today this structure is a visual reminder of why Hitler, a man who had convinced the German people that he was the leader who would build a German empire that was to last a thousand years, could not even finish building Congress Hall."

I still didn't get what Juri was going on about, but then Flo flashed me one of her frosty glares, so I said, "Okay, Let's go."

Juri drove around the Nazi Colosseum to a spot where he made a sharp right turn and everything looked different. "Now we are inside the Congress Hall. As you can see, the structure was halted because the Nazi party ran out of money."

Juri stopped the car. Me and Flo got out and looked around. I don't know how to tell you what I saw, except, the inside of the whole damn place was nothing more than a giant shell of a building. Like, if you've ever seen a movie where there's a big building. Hell, from your seat in the theater, the building looks rock-solid, like a real building. But if you could walk around to the other side, you'd see there's no real building. Just a bunch of 2x4 studs holding up a fake front.

I said, "Juri, this is the damnedest place I'd ever seen. The inside of this joint is nothing but brick wall. I mean me and Flo are staring at a ten-story high, unfinished, brick wall. Now I see what you meant. If that Hitler dude couldn't finish this building, how in the hell was he ever gonna finish a world war?"

Juri sighed, "Now you have it. Grandiose was the single architectural principle of the Nazi party. This structure is the only example of that extravagant principle that survives today."

I nodded, like I understood what the hell he was talking about and said, "Okay, what's next on the tour?"

"The Congress Hall shell where we are presently is just a small part of what was once called The Nazi Party Rally Grounds, or in German, the Reichsparteitagsgelände. The whole area covered many square kilometers in southeast of Nuremberg. The Rally Grounds included seven more unfinished or demolished structures that we do not have time for today. Now, I do not know about you, but there is a little stand just around the corner and I am ready for a cup of coffee."

I said, "Or a beer?"

"We'll drink a beer later. Right now, I need a cup of coffee. I go to bed very late and get up early because in addition to my assignment with you and Flo, I have to report to my office each day to work on my other cases."

Flo said, "Are you kidding me? Did you have to go to your office after you dropped us off at our hotel?

"I did."

I jumped in. "Okay, what about before you picked us up at the hotel this morning?"

"I was sitting at my desk as the sun rose over the horizon. What my body needs now is a large shot of caffeine."

Flo cried, "Juri, you work too hard."

Juri smiled, "I know, but I like my work."

While Juri talked, he drove me and Flo over to a little stand that served coffee and other stuff.

"My friends, please, sit down. I will pay for the coffee and if we are lucky, they will have a little something sweet to eat."

Me and Flo found a table with three chairs while Juri grabbed three cups of coffee and some little cookies.

"Babe, this dude is a nice guy. Do you think we should tell him we know the book is with Pinky on its way to Germany?"

Before Flo could answer Juri returned with the goods. The kid was right. The coffee and cookies hit the spot.

When he set down his empty cup, Juri said, "Now I believe we are ready to visit Zeppelin Field."

Flo said, "Juri, before we go, Bear and I want to thank you. During my university studies I dabbled with German history, but seeing the Congress Hall has given me a much better understanding into the insanity of Hitler's Third Reich."

Juri nodded. "Thank you, Flo. Then the people of Nuremberg have accomplished their goal by making this site a protected monument in 1973."

Flo said, "Okay, let's head to Zeppelin Field. After that we'll find a place where we can buy you a beer in appreciation of your kindness."

Juri smiled. "Good idea. Everyone back in the car. Zeppelin Field is close by."

As we walked back to Juri's car, I felt a little shitty 'cause Juri's been straight with us while we've known where the Altersomething book was since we landed in Nuremberg, and it wasn't in Germany! If I asked Pinky, he would tell me that we were doing the right thing, keeping quiet about the book; but lying through my teeth, like Pinky does all the time, is not the way me and Flo like to do things. Now, before you get your skivvies all twisted up, I know we've had to fudge the truth now and again, but not all the time, and sure as hell not when the guy we're working with was a straight-up dude like Juri.

It didn't take me long to figure out that Juri was right about the short drive to Zeppelin Field. I'd hardly got my seat belt clicked when it was time to get out of the car. This time we weren't looking at a big unfinished building. Zeppelin Field looked to me like a super, giant, football field with some old concrete grandstands stuck on one side.

As we walked toward the grandstands, a bus rolled by and we heard a dude on a

180

loudspeaker talking to a load of tourists riding inside.

"Babe, what language was that?"

"It's French."

Juri said, "That is correct, Flo. I did not know you speak French."

"I don't, but I can understand a bit."

After we let the bus pass, we crossed the road and started climbing up some tired looking concrete stairs. Juri kept us going until we got to a flat spot in the middle where we could stand and see everything below. Juri pointed at the huge field, like bigger than three or four football fields wide and a couple of football fields deep.

He said, "That giant expanse of grass in front of you is Zeppelin Field. Construction began in 1933 and was completed in 1937. This whole area was designed by Albert Speer for Hitler to hold spectacular rallies. For example, Hitler would tell his Nazi followers to assemble. Below where we stand a 100,000 brown-shirted men would cover the green grass. Movies were shot here in a way that made viewers all over the world feel the overwhelming power and might of the Nazi party. During nighttime events, firebrands and sophisticated lighting endowed the Zeppelin Field with an almost church-like atmosphere."

The sun was making me squint so I held my hand over my eyes as I looked around. I recalled seeing old newsreels about Nazi Germany. "Juri, is this the place where all the Nazis marched around with flags covered with swastikas while Hitler stood right here and acted like he was damn sure he was the king of the world?"

"You are correct. The three of us are standing on the exact rostrum where Hitler stood. The area you and Flo see below is where hundreds of thousands stood and cheered Hitler's rants."

Then Juri pointed. "Way out there, you can see the first of thirty-four concrete buildings."

Both me and Flo's eyes followed Juri's finger.

He said, "That concrete building on the left is the first of thirty-four identical structures spread out in a large arc that defines the back boundary of the Zeppelin Field. And on the roof of each concrete building, if you look closely, you will see six flag standards. Just imagine, the year is 1938. You are standing next to Hitler staring out at a hundred thousand uniformed party members. Then, just beyond Hitler's supporters you see an arc of thirty-four concrete structures topped with 204 giant red Nazi flags flying above the buildings."

I said, "Hold on, Juri. Are you telling me that those thirty-four buildings were built just to hold up six flags?"

"No, Bear. They were not built just to hold flags. They contained toilets for the masses who attended the rallies."

That Speer dude took an empty field, thirty-four concrete shit houses, topped them with flags, and turned this place into something that damn near helped Hitler win the war. Up 'til now, all I really knew about World War II and the Nazis, was what I'd seen in the movies and some old TV shows. I was really glad that Juri took me and Flo to see this place. I mean between Congress Hall and the Zeppelin Field, I was beginning to see how easy it was for the Germans to believe the bullshit that Hitler dished out.

I was ready to head back to the car when Flo piped up. "Juri, when I was just a young girl I recall seeing a film on TV that showed a Nazi rally held here at night and there were a bunch of searchlights that pointed straight up into the sky."

"I had almost forgotten about the search lights, Flo. Albert Speer designed special lighting effects that included 120 searchlights that shot their beams hundreds of feet into the sky. You also might be interested to know that Leni Riefenstahl, the famous German film maker, was probably responsible for the film you saw on television."

My Babe shook her head. "Stop right there. I've read more than I want to know about Leni Riefenstahl. I know how she took gypsies out of concentration camps and used them to make her propaganda movies. Once she was finished making the movie, she would send them back to the concentration camps, some to their eventual death in gas chambers. Leni claimed that she didn't know that they were from concentration camps, but I don't believe that. And there's that quote that's attributed to her, 'To me, Hitler is the greatest man who ever lived. He truly is without fault, so simple and at the same time possessed of masculine strength.' I'm sorry, Juri, my guess is that when you mentioned Leni Riefenstahl you were trying to reach my feminine side. But female or male, a Nazi is still a Nazi, so if you want to remain my friend, don't ever mention her name to me again!"

I could tell that Juri got a little bent out of shape when Flo cut him a new one, so I said, "Okay, how 'bout we find a place where I can order us a beer in German?"

After a couple more seconds of trying to figure out if he should fire back at Flo, or agree with me, Juri finally flashed me a smile. "Bear, are you sure you know how to order three beers?"

Damn, I'll bet what he taught me only works for one beer. "Okay what do I say for three beers?"

"Drei bier, Bitte."

"So dry means three, right?"

Juri nodded. "Ja."

"Got it."

We jumped into Juri's car and inside of ten minutes we were sitting around a table at Juri's favorite beer bar. Me and Juri had giant mugs of some really super beer, while Flo worked on a glass of white wine. Why she would drink wine instead of a good, cold beer was something I could never figure out.

After a couple of lady-like sips, she flashed me a look that told me something was coming. "Juri, we know your boss thinks that Helmut Kaufmann murdered his uncle, but we know for a fact that's wrong."

Juri stopped drinking his beer and set the mug down. "Okay, how do you know that Helmut Kaufmann did not kill his uncle?"

"How do we know that? Because he lacked the motive to murder his uncle."

Juri glanced at me, then Flo, and his face had that look I'd seen before, just before a cop threw the cuffs on me. "And how are you so sure of that?"

Flo flashed Juri a look that could melt the icicles off an Igloo. "Because two weeks before the murder took place in Nuremberg, Helmut's uncle FedExed the book to Helmut's home in Carson City."

I said, "Last night, Flo got an email from our boss, Pinky. He's flying to Nuremberg this evening. Besides himself, he's bringing the book you've been looking for, that old Achleadersomething. See, that's way me and Flo are positive that Helmut Kaufmann is innocent."

Juri picked up his beer, started to gulp some down and then he stopped. That worried me 'cause a guy doesn't stop drinking until his glass is empty. He stared at me, then Flo, and I don't mean just her boobs, like he was hoping to find something, anything that told him it was okay to trust a couple of dumb Americans. For a few seconds you could almost see his brain putting the loose ends together and then he looked like he was thinking about getting up and walking out. Finally he said, "How long have you two known the book was in America?"

I jumped up and said, "Juri, me and Flo know we did a chicken-shit thing by not telling you we knew where the book was."

As the pissed-off look on his face continued, Juri said, "So you both knew the book was in the U.S. before you landed in Nuremberg?"

Flo said, "We should have told you about the book before, but as soon as Pinky emailed us that he was flying to Nuremberg, with the book, we knew we had to tell you the truth."

Juri didn't say anything and for a second I thought he was going to throw cuffs on both of us. He glanced at me, and then Flo, and using his bad cop voice, he growled, "Frau Florence, Herr Bear, you have not answered my question. One more time, did you know that the Achtliederbuch was in America when you landed in Nuremberg?"

Me and Flo just sort of sat there and didn't say anything.

Juri's voice got a little louder. "I will even make my question less complex. Did you know that the book was in the United Sates while the three of us wasted my valuable afternoon searching for the Achtliederbuch in the Kaufmann bookshop?"

My Babe flashed Juri a look that sorta told him she was sorry, and then she nodded.

Now his face slipped into a totally pissed off look. I guess he'd thought that Flo would do the right thing. "Madam, your blatant deception changes everything."

I moved real close to my Babe so I could slow Juri down in case he was about to drag us off to the local slam.

I said, "Cool down, Juri. Just like Flo said, we didn't know Pinky was bringing the book with him 'til last night."

Juri exclaimed, "You told me that before. When we met in Nuremberg that first morning at your hotel you both knew the book was in the United States, not Germany. Am I correct?"

Flo said, "You are. Obviously, we have not been completely honest with you."

"Frau Florence, my command of English is not perfect, but for you to claim you have not been completely honest with me would be interpreted as a classic understatement in English or German."

I wasn't a hundred percent sure what all that understatement crap was about, but I sure as hell could tell that Juri was really pissed off.

I had to try and talk him down. "Juri, you're right about what we told you. And I agree with you that what me and Flo did was really chicken shit. From now on, I promise we'll be totally straight with you. And to prove it, I'm going to buy us another round."

Flo started talking before Juri had the chance to tell me that buying a couple of beers wasn't going to get us out of this mess. "Bear's right. But we had a legal and ethical reason to do what we did. First, we had an obligation to our client, Helmut Kaufmann, to get him off your boss's shit list. We knew Helmut was innocent long before we flew to Nuremberg because the Achtliederbuch arrived by FedEX a week before Helmut left America."

Juri sat back, like he was trying to figure out if Flo was feeding him the straight skinny or just another bucket of bullshit. Then he said, "Do you have proof that Helmut possessed the book in America, before he flew to Nuremberg?"

Not sure if dorky old Helmut had kept his FedEx receipt, I was about to say most anything when Flo jumped in. "Both Helmut and FedEx have records of the shipment. In fact, FedEx will have a record of the shipment even if the date isn't on the box."

Juri nodded. "Flo, you are correct. FedEx tracks all their shipments. I can get proof of the date of delivery from them."

I nodded my head up and down, like he'd get the FedEx tracking info tomorrow. But as I thought about it, me and Flo really didn't have anything more than Helmut's word. That's when old Grandpas Zabarte's words about how to bluff in a poker game came to me. I was about sixteen, just starting to get into penny-ante games, when Grandpa told me, "Bear, if you're dealt a shitty hand, just don't do something stupid and pull a pissed-off face. All that does is tell the other players around the table that your five cards are crappy. My boy, you were born with a giant pair of cajones, so you shove all your chips into the center of the table like you've got a royal flush. Now all that's left to do is say, "All in."

Following my Grandpa's advice, I went all in. "Juri, the first time we met you told us that you didn't believe that Helmut strangled his uncle. What you needed was to find the book so you could dangle it, like bait on a rat trap, to get those new-Nazis out of their hiding place. From that day, me and Flo knew our job was to convince our boss to bring the book to Nuremberg. Pinky's plane lands in a little while and he's got the book! So me and Flo apologize for leading you down a bull-shit alley. Real soon you'll be holding the book—the book you've been looking for—in your hands."

For a while, Juri didn't say anything, so I jumped up, grabbed the mugs, Flo's wine glass, and headed to the bar. The babe behind the bar who had a pair almost as big as Flo's, stood there like she was waiting for me to order. I said,"Dry beer, and wine, bit."

She looked at the two mugs I set down, shook her head and held up two fingers. I nodded. While she filled the mugs and poured some wine into Flo's glass, I figured out that I had ordered dry beer. Hell, dry's three, not two.

Everybody knows that! Lucky for me she was smarter than I was. By the time I headed back to the table, Flo was jawing with Juri and I could see by his smile that Grandpa's bluff had worked again.

Flo took her glass from my little finger and I set the mugs down. I looked back in the direction of the bar and I spotted a few little puddles of beer on the floor.

"Juri, you taught me that dry in German is three, but how do you say two?"

"Zwei."

"Like swhy."

Juri looked at me, like I was trying to make fun or something. Then he said, "Not exactly. You need to give the w of the why a little more v after the s sound."

"Huh?"

Flo jumped in. "Juri, I'd give up if I were you. I'm amazed you got Bear to say swhy."

Juri nodded. "I understand. Now, one other observation. Bear, everyone in this establishment can see and hear that you know how to order beers and one wine, but ..." He glanced at the beer I'd spilled on the floor. "You need a little more work on carrying the beer back to the table." He took a big sip, set his mug down, and said, "Flo, Bear, I have to admit I am still a little upset that you withheld critical information concerning the Kaufmann

191

murder. And this is even more important, that you knew the Achtliederbuch was in America and did not tell me." Juri downed another slug. "However, I will accept your apology, but from this point on, you two will not hold anything back. No more secrets! From now on we are three colleagues working toward the common goal of finding and arresting the killers of Konrad Kaufmann. Do we all agree?"

As Juri lifted his mug, I gave a little wink to Grandpa Zabarte for teaching me about bluffing. Flo lifted her glass. Then I followed with my mug. Me and Juri downed some beer and Flo sipped wine. Then we yelled, "Agreed!"

Then Juri glanced at his watch and jumped up. "What time did you say your boss's flight arrives?"

Flo , after she emptied her glass of wine, said, "Around six-fifteen. Why?"

Juri slammed his empty mug onto the table. "Damn. Comrades, the airport is a ten-minute drive and according to my watch it is now six-twenty. I will call for a cab because it would not look good for a detective assigned to the Kriminalpolizei section of the Bavarian State Police to be pulled over for driving to the airport under the influence of three beers worth of alcohol."

Chapter Twenty-One

Pinky Delmont—Nuremberg, Germany

As the plane banked to begin our approach to Nuremberg, I had mentally started a letter of complaint to KLM for the cramped seating arrangement on their Embraer 175, the aircraft for the final leg of my journey. Granted, the flight was only seventy minutes long, but I had paid handsomely for a business class seat. The section of the plane that they called KLM Europe Select did not come close to a genuine business class accommodation. And to top KLM's gross misnomer, my seat, 4C, was next to a very large male who easily weighed over two hundred and fifty pounds, so I spent most of the seventy minutes leaning into the aisle, placing my right shoulder directly into the flight attendant's line of fire.

Once the wheels touched down, I made myself an unconditional promise to file a suit of false advertising against KLM and demand they compensate me for this leg, and the identical leg during my return flight home.

As my baggage consisted of a single briefcase, I ignored the luggage carousel that belched out an endless line of large and small suitcases of all colors, sizes, and shapes, and made my way to the passport check point.

After a uniformed officer stamped my passport, I followed the arrows on the floor to the exit where I expected to find Bear and Florence, dutifully waiting for my arrival.

However, when I reached a large area with forty to fifty persons eagerly scanning the faces of the arriving passengers, neither Bear nor Florence was among the crowd. Cursing under my breath, I made my way through the assemblage to the sidewalk just as a cab pulled up to the curb. Bear and Florence jumped out with big smiles pasted across their faces.

"Hi, boss."

"Bear, Florence, had I waited on the sidewalk ten seconds longer, I would have been forced to reduce your salary by ten percent."

"Sorry, boss, but—"

Doing my best to ignore the crowd jostling behind me, I demanded, "No buts. Why were you so late?"

"You see, me and Flo—"

The throng behind me was so eager to catch a taxi that they pushed me into the two. I demanded, "Bear, is that beer I smell on your breath?"

Taken aback by my accusation, he struggled to find a response, I cried, "Don't destroy any more brain cells trying to compose a response. Is that my cab?"

"Ah . . . Yes, boss."

"Well, don't just stand there. Open the door."

Bear opened the back door. When I waved Florence in I glanced inside and across the seat sat a man I did not recognize. I slipped into the taxi next to Florence and said, "Florence, having just endured an extremely long journey trapped in business class I am exhausted."

After Bear climbed into the front seat next to the driver, Florence asked, "Where's your baggage?"

"I left rather abruptly. Florence, once I am ensconced in a hotel room, I trust you will go out and purchase me a toothbrush."

The vixen said, "No need to buy a toothbrush or toothpaste. Your hotel will supply those. But you're going to come up short concerning fresh underwear and socks. First question, boxers or briefs?"

"Boxers."

"Got it. Next, I'll need to know your waist measurement. Most socks should fit your puny feet."

I glanced at the unknown man sitting next to Florence, but too tired to argue about sharing my vital statistics with a stranger I said, "Thirty-two waist and size eight shoe.

Now that everyone, including the taxi driver is aware of my waist and shoe size, Florence, does that man sitting next to you have a name?"

He nodded, leaned across Florence's ample bosom, and offered his hand. "Juri Vogel, Detective of the Kriminalpolizei section of the Bavarian State Police. And you are Attorney Delmont?"

"Yes, I am, Detective. But in the future, I would prefer you address me as Pinky."

Vogel shook his head and smiled, "First it is Bear, then Flo, now Pinky. In Germany, I would never consider addressing an attorney I just met by a nickname. However, your request reminds me that the customs of America are quite different than those of my country."

"Detective Vogel, hopefully my stay in Nuremberg will be brief, so I am not at all interested in the differences of our two countries' customs."

Florence jabbed her elbow into my side. "Pinky, ease up. Juri's on our side. He's positive the prime suspect for the Kaufmann murder was not his nephew, Helmut."

At this point in time, all I wanted to do was find a hotel and crawl into bed. But Florence's statement forced my mind to ask a final question. "Detective Vogel, if not Helmut Kaufmann, than who?"

From the front seat of the taxi Bear said, "He thinks a gang of new-Nazis murdered Konrad Kaufmann for the Achtersomething, the book you brought with you."

Florence said, "Pinky, you should be overjoyed to meet the one German cop who believes your client is innocent."

Florence directed her last comment to me. However, my journey from Las Vegas to Nuremberg, with stopovers in Minneapolis and Amsterdam, had taken its toll on my mind and body. And I found it impossible to be overjoyed about anything. In fact, all I wanted to do was lay down on a bed, stretch out my limbs, and close my eyes.

"Detective Vogel, assuming what Florence just told me concerning your view of my client is correct, what do you need from me?"

"Pinky, all I need from you is the Achtliederbuch. Presumably the book is inside the briefcase you hold in your lap?"

I moved my briefcase away from him, and said, "Detective Vogel—"

The detective interrupted, "Excuse me. I will continue to address you as Pinky, as long as you call me Juri. If not, I will revert back to the formal Herr Delmont."

A loud buzzing inside my head was interrupting my ability to concentrate. I was exhausted. I was trapped inside a German cab that I hoped would take me to a soft bed in a quiet hotel room. Simply stated, my tank of energy was nearly empty. I glanced left toward the window and the darkening sky. "Juri, I have never been able to fall asleep during a flight, and I did not sleep at all during the twelve hours prior to boarding the plane in Las Vegas. I need you to take me to my hotel. Tomorrow morning, after a full night's rest, I will discuss the book with you."

Juri said, "Excellent. Flo, after you left the cab I called The Sorat Hotel, the same hotel where you and Bear are staying. All standard rooms were booked but they did have a suite available, so I booked the suite for three nights. Your boss can extend his stay beyond the three nights if he feels the need. Once we get him checked in, and escort him to his room, I will accompany you to Karstadt, the finest department store in Nuremberg, where you will be able to purchase the clothing items Pinky requires."

Nearly asleep on my feet, we arrived at the hotel. While standing in the lobby to check in, my knees almost gave way as I gave Florence my final instructions. "Florence, when you check me in, ask for two keys and then immediately take me to my room. Later, after you have purchased all the agreed upon items of clothing, you have my permission to enter my room and leave the extra key on top of my new clothing."

Florence responded. "Gotcha. Now let's get you upstairs and into bed."

Five minutes later, finally alone in my room, I crawled into bed and placed my head on the soft down pillow. I had extinguished the lights and the room was quiet. However, in spite of my efforts to shut down my brain, I could not turn off the stark images of my previous thirty hours—Tonopah—Las Vegas—Smith's Hardware—Denny's—McCarran Airport—the never-ending drone of jet engines.

Eventually, my mind shut down and a much-needed sleep followed.

Chapter Twenty-Two

Bear Zabarte—Nuremberg, Germany

After we got Pinky into his room, Juri and Flo left to buy the boss some skivvies so I had time to hit the mini-bar in our room for some beer while I tried to find the Sox baseball game, hell, any baseball game on our dumb TV. After the second beer I gave up looking and hustled down to the lobby to find out what the hell was going on with my TV.

The same snooty dude that checked us in a couple of days ago was standing behind the desk. As I walked up, he said, "May I help you?"

"Hey, our room is good. The mini-bar is great, but I can't find the Red Sox game on your stupid TV."

He gave me his I-don't-know-what-the-hell-you're-talking-about face.

Then I remembered I was in Germany, not Carson City, and maybe the dude doesn't understand English real well, so I slowed way down, and said, "Dude...I...can't...find...the... Boston...Red...Sox...game...on...the...stupid... room...TV."

"Sir, I understand English. What I did not understand was your question. First, please give me your room number."

"Room 312, and my name is Bear, not sir."

"Mr. Bear, I will send a technician to room 312 at once to fix your TV."

"Dude, you still don't understand. The TV works fine. I just can't find my favorite baseball team, the Boston Red Sox, on any of the fifty channels. The Sox are in the playoffs and it's gotta be on TV. Every game is important, no matter what Flo says."

The dude's nose kinda scrunched up, like one of us just farted. Then he said, "My name is Karl, not Dude. Mr. Bear, are you talking about watching an American Baseball game on the television in your room?"

Now we were getting somewhere. "Karl, you've got it. You see, the Boston Red Sox are part of the American League. After they win this playoff series they'll be playing a team from the National League. Now, I know my Sox are a much better team then—"

"Mr. Bear, I apologize, but you are in Nuremberg, Germany, and our television providers do not offer any American baseball games. Perhaps there's a bar, I believe you call them sport bars, in town."

"So Karl, let me get this straight. You're telling me that I can't get my Sox games in any room in this hotel? Is that right?"

"Correct. But I have an idea, Mr. Bear. Do you own a smart phone?"

"I do. My boss gives me a new one each year so he can keep track of me. You see, my boss doesn't trust me as far as he can throw me."

"I see. Do you have your phone with you?"

"Yup." I pulled my iPhone out of my back pocket. "Don't go anywhere without it. Why?"

"Would you be so kind as to hand your phone to me for a moment?"

"Hell yes." I gave my phone to the dude. "Whatcha going to do?"

The dude, sorry, Karl, turned the phone toward my face. I heard a little click. Then he fiddled farted around for a minute. Then he handed the phone back to me.

"Mr. Bear, I just used your phone's Face ID to unlock the phone. Then, on a hunch, I downloaded the MLB App onto your phone. From now on, no matter where you are, as long as you have cell service, or can receive wireless, just open the app, find the Red Sox game, and you will be able to watch it."

"Wow! Karl, thanks. I can hardly wait tell Flo that I can watch my team play ball when we're in bed, or I'm perched on the john. You know, when we checked in, I thought you were a kinda snooty dude, Karl. But I was wrong. You're a straight-up guy."

Again, Karl shot me his I-don't-know-what-the-hell-you're-talking-about face again. Then he said, "You are most welcome, Mr. Bear. Now, if I have resolved your problem to your satisfaction, please excuse me. I have other pressing duties."

I glanced around the lobby and didn't spot anybody waiting at the check-in counter. Just between you and me, I think the dude was hoping I'd move on. Go to my room. Go to the bar. Go anywhere but the front desk.

I said, "No problem. Hey, I owe you a beer." But I don't think he heard me about the beer 'cause he was typing away on a keyboard.

I went back to my room, pulled another beer out of the little refrigerator and I was just in time to watch my Sox squeak out a win in the ninth inning of the fifth game of the playoffs.

Chapter Twenty-Three

Pinky Delmont—Nuremberg, Germany

The fog of sleep slowly lifted as the loud siren of an emergency vehicle racing through the street below my room stimulated the neurons in my brain. I gently opened my eyes and rapidly snapped them closed once the startling rays of sunshine hit my retinas.

Squinting, I lifted myself out of bed, shuffled my way to the windows and closed the drapes.

Once the outside light had been diminished, I looked around my room for the first time. If memory served me, I recalled the young detective told me he had booked me into a suite. The space I stood in was an L-shaped room, and not, under any circumstances, expansive enough to be designated as a suite. Granted, the room did have five large windows that overlooked an open-air marketplace and a distinctive church, but a good view did not make up for the lack of a separate room that in my experience was required to designate a hotel room a suite.

I turned and spotted a chair against the far wall. On the chair were six pair of gray boxer shorts, a dozen pairs of black socks, and my second room key.

I was pleased to note that Florence and that young detective, Juri, had followed my clothing directive to the letter. Under those extenuating circumstances, I decided not to rebuke the young detective for failing to book me into a proper suite.

I picked up a fresh pair of boxers and a pair of socks, and was on my way to a much-needed shower when my room phone rang.

"Hello?"

"Hi, boss. How's it hanging? Me and Flo are about ready to head downstairs for breakfast. Boss, you've got to see it to believe it! This joint has one of the greatest breakfast spreads in the world."

"Bear, I was about to step into the shower. Once I have completed that task, I will join you downstairs for breakfast. Also, tell Florence to send an email to Robert to inform him I have safely arrived in Nuremberg. By the way, what day is it?"

"It's Monday."

"Fine. Include in the message of my arrival, have Florence tell Robert to book me a return flight to Reno for Wednesday. The booking must be first class with no more than a three-hour layover between any of the flights. Did you get that?"

"Huh, I think so. You said Wednesday, and no more than three hours layover, and one more thing, but I can't remember."

"First class, you dolt."

"Gotcha, boss. I'll tell Flo to do that as soon as I hang up."

Forty minutes later, as I entered the dining room, my olfactory organs were pleasantly tantalized by the delicious aroma of freshly brewed coffee. As I gazed at the appetizing display of breakfast items, I realized I had not consumed real food for more than twenty-four hours. While I ambled down the buffet line placing various cheeses and meats onto my plate, Bear joined me.

"Boss, once you've got that plate filled, you gotta sit at me and Flo's table. Don't forget to grab a couple of hunks of that dark bread. There's a pot of strawberry jam sitting on each table and a bowl full of the best butter you ever tasted."

Satisfied I had picked up enough food to fill my empty void, I found their table and sat down. While I consumed my repast, Florence and I exchanged an occasional nod. I agreed with Bear, this hotel had an outstanding breakfast buffet. Also, I should have taken a second slice of bread, a wonderful carrier for that outstanding butter and strawberry jam.

While I sat back and enjoyed my second cup of coffee, Florence said, "Pinky, Juri will be here soon, so tell us why you decided to come to Nuremberg and how come you didn't sell your book?"

"Florence, this is no time to dwell on the past. We need to concentrate on the future. Tell me, now that I have arrived in Nuremberg do you have a plan."

Florence said, "That book's an integral part of our plan. You brought it with you, right?"

"Of course I did. Did you think I would fly thousands of miles just to break bread with you? Go ahead, what is your plan?"

Bear said, "Boss, speaking of bread, I was right about that strawberry jam! And how about the—"

The two were after me as if I were a bowl of honey and they were bees. I snapped, "Bear, contain your remarks to the subject being discussed. Go ahead Florence."

She brought me up to speed concerning everything that had happened since they arrived in Nuremberg.

I was about to remark on how little they had accomplished when Juri appeared and joined our table.

"Good morning, Herr Delmont.

I shook my head. "I thought we agreed last night to keep this informal. In the future, you will address me as Pinky."

Juri responded, "As you requested, Pinky. Now, do you have the book in your room?"

"I do. But first, I need an explanation as to what you plan to do with my book."

Juri said, "As you heard last night, "I believe that the prime suspect for the Kaufmann murder is part of a neo-Nazi cell located in Nuremberg. My plan is to offer them the opportunity to purchase your book to flush them out of their hiding place."

I snorted, "Offer my book to a gang of murderers? My good man, before this discussion goes any further, we need to come to an agreement. The book remains in my possession at all times. If your neo-Nazis want to look at the book, I must be present."

Juri shook his head. "But Pinky, you are talking about the men who murdered Konrad Kaufmann. Killing an American attorney for the book would mean nothing to them."

Bear interrupted. "Hey, maybe I could go along with Pinky. To sorta protect him."

Juri shook his head. "Sorry, Bear. But a man of your size might present a danger to them. And I can't accompany him because the criminal class of this city knows who I am."

I sat back and nodded in the direction of Florence. "How about Florence? Trust me, Juri, she can be a formidable force when the occasion arises."

She shrugged. "As long as Bear and Juri know where we are, I'm game."

Bear growled, "But what happens if we lose sight of you and Pinky. What will you do then?"

Florence said, "I'm confident that you two can follow us. Juri, don't you cops have some sort of tracking devices you can put on Pinky and me?"

Juri didn't answer for a moment, and that should have warned me that something about the tracking devices was bothering him. Then he nodded. "Yes, I can wire you both up and track your every move, but I agree with Bear. There is a high risk that something could go wrong."

Pinky said, "Why do you say that?"

"Because Nuremberg is a large urban area of roughly a half a million people. We are not talking about keeping track of you in a small country village. This is a very big and old city with many underground tunnels and passageways."

I took my final sip of coffee and said, "Detective, presently this is Monday morning. I am leaving Nuremberg, with my book, on

Wednesday. That means you have today and tomorrow to get Florence and myself wired up with your tracking device and set up the meeting with your Nazi miscreants."

Juri smiled. "I will contact you both once I have secured the devices and arranged the meeting."

Juri jumped up and left the dining room.

I said, "Florence, after I brush my teeth, I would appreciate if you would accompany me to that department store where you purchased those clothing items for me. Considering I flew here with the clothes on my back, I am in the market for a pair of slacks, two shirts, and a sweater for my return flight home."

Chapter Twenty-Four

Pinky Delmont—Nuremberg, Germany

After breakfast I returned to my room. A moment after my door closed, my cell phone rang.

I answered it and snapped, "Florence, I said we would meet in the lobby in half an hour."

"Pinky, this is not Florence. This is the guardian of your gate, Robert V. Silva."

I glanced at my watch which showed 9:45 am. Considering the time difference, it was forty-five minutes after midnight in Carson City. Concerned that my majordomo might be angling for overtime pay, I responded, "Robert, as I did not authorize you to work outside your normal office hours, unless this call is a matter of life or death, you should hang up and go to bed."

"Pinky, this is a matter of life or death and as long as you remain in Germany, that life could be mine."

In the brief time that Robert had worked for me he had never exhibited a tendency toward hyperbole. With a rising level of angst, I asked, "What has happened?"

"Two words—Hook Dudek. That man marched into the office and before I could lift the receiver to call the police, he buried that damn hook into the center of my phone."

Perhaps I could extend my visit to Germany. "Robert, I am grateful that beyond the damage to the office phone, Hook did not do you any physical harm."

"Pinky, for thirty years I lived and worked in San Francisco with all the expected crime and violence. Once I moved to Carson City, I thought I had left all that behind me. But today, I actually experienced real fear for my life from a colleague of yours!"

I said, "Robert, I contacted you and warned you that—"

Robert screamed, "It's too late for a warning. That man's a maniac with a lethal weapon attached to his arm."

"My good man, calm down and tell me what happened."

The line was quiet for a moment, as if Robert needed a few moments to cease hyperventilating.

"Pinky, here's what happened. Hook barged into the office a few minutes before closing. After his hook had destroyed my phone, he then used it to demolish the copy machine and finally the printer. Lucky, by that time his anger had vented to the point that I felt I was not going to be his next target. Pinky, he claimed that after you drove him to Las Vegas, you vanished and left him sitting in a coffee shop with no way to return to Carson City."

My mind raced to find a reasonable explanation for my abrupt and unexpected action. "He is correct, Robert. I did abandon Hook that morning, However, you only have his side of the story. While I was using the facility, I received a call from an important client in Germany. That is why I called you to make flight reservations to Nuremberg, Germany. And do not forget that I told you to pay Hook his ten thousand dollar finder's fee plus an extra five thousand for his trouble."

Again, there was a pause before Robert responded, but this time I felt he was weighing the veracity of my reason for abandoning Hook.

"I did cut the man a check for $15,000, but even that amount of money didn't come close to reducing his anger toward you. What really seemed to piss him off was that he felt he had lost the respect of an associate, the man the two of you drove to Las Vegas to meet."

"Robert, I'll be home in two days."

"Pinky, I'm sorry but—"

I interrupted him, "And if Hook returns, call the police. In fact, the moment you enter the office tomorrow morning call the police. Show them the damage Hook has done to my office equipment and then—"

"PINKY, SHUT UP AND LET ME FINISH! I've thought about this for hours, ever since I closed up your office. You'll have to find another sucker to make your reservations and deal with the police. As of this moment, I quit. I've packed up my few belongings and I'm moving back to peaceful San Francisco. I'd like to say working for you was fun, but it wasn't."

I heard a click and Robert was gone. Not just from the call, but from my professional life. And as the time in Carson City was approaching 1:00 am, I would not be able to call Loomer for Silva's replacement for another eight hours. Not sure what to do next, I walked to my picture window and stared at the people walking in the plaza below. Suddenly my room phone rang.

Could it be Robert apologizing for his crass remarks and begging for his job back?. With a hint of satisfaction, I lifted the receiver. "Robert, is this you?"

"Damn it Pinky, I've been waiting for you in the lobby for the last ten minutes. Are we going to the store or not?"

Florence! I was about to verbally chastise her for cursing at me, but then I realized she was the solution to my present dilemma. During our little shopping expedition I would have time to bring her up to date concerning the cowardly exit of my former majordomo, Robert V. Silva. And how she, as my full-time employee, could act in my stead and work over the phone with Loomer for an immediate replacement.

"Something unexpected happened. I'll meet you in the lobby and bring you up to date in five minutes."

Chapter Twenty-Five

Bear Zabarte—Nuremberg, Germany

A couple of hours after Flo left for her shopping spree, I was sitting in my room, trying to figure out what time the next Sox game came on my phone, when my cell chirped.

"Hello?"

"Hi, Bear. Juri here. Are Flo and Pinky with you?"

"Nope."

"Do you expect them soon?"

"Don't know. If I know my Babe, and I do know my Babe, once she gets near the broad's clothes section inside a department store all bets are off. Why?"

"I have signed out the tracking devices. All I have left to do is to set up the meeting with my man."

I sat up. This was a good time for me to tell Juri that letting Flo and Pinky run off with a bunch of new-Nazis was a bad idea. Hell, I didn't give a damn about Pinky. He's so nasty I don't think anyone out there would want to get close enough to kill him. But my Babe, she's another kettle of fish. Flo acts tough, like trouble pours off her like water off a duck's back, but most of that bristle is an act.

"Juri, I don't wanna have Flo wander around Nuremberg with a bunch of new-Nazis and Pinky as her only way out of trouble."

"I share your concern, but when the neo-Nazis reach for the bait, I am confident that we will be right there. Like I said before, all that I need to do now is contact my inside man."

"You've got a guy who'll fink on the new-Nazis?"

Juri chuckled. "Yes, but I call him my man. He will set up the time and place for Pinky and Flo to meet with the neo-Nazis."

"And you me will be with right behind them, right?"

"Right."

My door popped open and my Babe and Pinky waltzed in.

I said, "Juri, you'd better head over to our hotel right now 'cause Flo and Pinky are here and they're ready to go."

"I will be there as soon as I make the arrangements."

I walked over to that cool little refrigerator, pulled out a beer, and popped the top. "Babe, Pinky, Juri's setting up the meeting with his guy and he'll join us here once he's got everything lined up."

Pinky said, "A true gentleman would have offered a beer to everyone in the room."

Shit! "Okay, anybody besides me want a brew?"

Flo shook her head while Pinky said, "Drinking beer straight out of the bottle is beneath my standards. If you can't pour the liquid amber into a glass just forget it."

I flashed Pinky my nastiest glare and was about to tell him to pound salt when Flo said, "Hold on, Bear. I'll get Pinky a clean glass from the bathroom."

While I poured the dork some beer, he said, "One thing we must make clear to Detective Vogel is that I will not ever let the book out of my grasp under any circumstances."

That was when I almost poured the beer over his head. I'd had it with Pinky and his Achtersomething. "Boss, you sent me and Flo to Nuremberg to come up with a patsy for the German cops so your client would get dropped off their shit list. We've done our job so no matter what happens the rest of this day, me and Flo are heading back to Carson City as soon as we can get a plane reservation. Just so me and you are clear, if that means that your book ends up in the sewer, I don't give a damn 'cause sometimes shit just happens!"

Pinky made a move toward me, like he was actually thinking about throwing a punch. All this time we've worked together, I thought he was too smart to do something that dumb. I grabbed his hand before it reached me and started to squeeze it hard enough to get juice out of a rock. Pinky's eyes opened wide and he was about to cry like a baby when we heard a knock at the door.

Flo grabbed my arm. "Calm down Bear. You don't want to do anything that will affect our future."

I relaxed my grip on Pinky's hand. Flo opened the door and Juri walked in.

Chapter Twenty-Six

Pinky Delmont—Nuremberg, Germany

As I struggled to endure the pain to my hand caused by my employee, I looked into Bear's angry eyes. It was obvious from his unwarranted attack that perhaps our generally tenuous relationship had finally come to an end.

Detective Vogel started going over his plan, but the pain from Bear's punishing grip blotted out most of his words. As he droned on, I made a mental note that the moment I returned home, I would begin my search for a new investigative team. The District Attorney's office had a small force of investigators, so perhaps Willow could offer me a few possibilities that—

As startling as an unexpected clap of thunder, Florence yelled, "Earth to Pinky, stop zoning out. Juri's plan involves all of us."

A touch embarrassed, I responded, "I have heard every word of Detective Vogel's plan. Please continue."

Juri said, "Okay, I have a tracking device for each of you. The first one is a fashionable pendant for Flo, and the other is a small black square that is about the size of a postage stamp for Pinky."

Florence, like all females, was immediately enamored by the jewelry look of the blue device. She smiled as she put it around her neck while I dropped the nondescript black square into my pants pocket.

"Next, and this is most important, at four this afternoon you will walk across the street and meet a man named Dieter at the Schöner Brunnen. Bear, in English that means beautiful fountain. The fountain is located in the Hauptmarkt square close to the town hall."

A puzzled look must have crossed my face because Detective Vogel said, "Come over to the window. You can see the fountain from here."

The three of us did as asked. Detective Vogel pointed down and said, "There is the fountain. Any questions?"

I said, "Yes, where do we go from the fountain?"

"That I do not know. That is why I have given you both tracking devices. After you meet Dieter, I am sure he will walk you across the plaza to another location. But you need not worry, Bear and I will be following right behind you."

I said, "So I have your assurance that the Bavarian State Police Department agrees there is no risk to my life concerning this little caper."

The Detective hesitated a fraction of a second, not a large gap of time, but long enough for an attorney who makes his living picking up tiny nuances to know the Detective was not being completely forthright.

Detective Vogel continued, "Pinky, as I said, Bear and I will be there if and when we are needed. Oh, I almost forgot to remind you that you must have the Achtliederbuch with you when you meet Dieter at the fountain."

"As you recall, Detective Vogel, I flew to Germany with my book so you could use it to expose the murderers of Konrad Hoffman. What sort of guarantee can you give me that the Achtliederbuch will not be taken from me?"

"As I previously stated, you have nothing to worry about. Bear and I will be tracking your every move and ready to step in as needed."

I glanced at my watch. It showed 3:30. "Florence, if we are to meet a gentleman named Dieter in thirty minutes, we need to get moving. I realize it is summer but once the sun sets I am sure the air will get cooler. I need to pick up a sweater from my room before we depart."

She replied, "Pinky, stop acting like a wimp. It's a warm, sunny day out there."

Chapter Twenty-Seven

Flo Sonderlund—Nuremberg, Germany

As Bear wasn't with us when we met Dieter in the Hauptmarkt, it's my job to report what happened once we met Juri's informant by the fountain.

I will get to that chronicle in a moment, but first, I need to tell you about a theory of mine that proved itself true during my earlier shopping trip with Pinky to buy him some clothes.

Once we arrived at the department store, Pinky pushed me toward a directory sign that showed the floors where the various departments were located. When he determined that the men's section was located on the second floor, Pinky stepped onto the escalator that took us to that floor where we entered the men's clothing department. Without glancing left or right, as if to shield his eyes from some artfully displayed clothing, he walked directly to a shelf piled high with men's pants. In no time his hands worked through a stack of khaki chinos, found his size, and draped a pair over his arm. Next, we wandered around until we found the sweater section, and again, with no thought to style or color he grabbed the first light brown sweater in his size. With those two items in hand, Pinky's shopping trip inside a famous German department store, an emporium that featured high fashion from around the world, an establishment he would likely never enter again, was complete. We paid at the nearest cash register and walked out of the store. The total time expended inside the establishment barely exceed ten minutes.

During my years with Bear, I had witnessed the identical congenital disorder each time I accompanied my man on his annual shopping trip to replace his threadbare, shabby clothing. Bear would make a beeline to the Levi's section, grab four pairs of jeans, a dozen shirts, and his wardrobe shopping was complete for another year.

Truthfully, Pinky's aversion to shopping goes to prove to my satisfaction that there is a genetic defect with all males, not just him.

Now that I've gotten the men's lack of style off my chest, I will bring you up to date concerning the outfit I wore that day:

A chic pair of navy slacks by Versace were fashionably paired with a powder blue silk blouse that was as soft as a morning breeze.

I topped off everything with my stylish dark-blue sapphire pendent tracking device that was a very classy piece of fake jewelry.

Pinky? The aforementioned pair of khaki chinos and a brown sweater on top of a white buttoned-down shirt—aka—the basic male uniform.

I've spent more than enough time on this subject, but it appalls me that men I have known spend so little thought concerning the clothing they wear.

Nor do they acknowledge a sparkling clear day.

Nor the first yellow of daffodils in spring.

I could go on and on, but I think you get my drift. Women seem to care more about making life a sublime experience rather than a dreadful slog. But enough of my personal theories. We've got some murderers to catch.

Pinky and I left the hotel and walked across the street through a brilliant afternoon sun to the Schöner Brunnen fountain where we met the man named Dieter.

The fountain was located in the upper left corner of the Hauptmarkt, a large open space used weekdays by farmers to market their produce. The sun was warm, but I noticed some ominous clouds on the eastern horizon that told me the day had the possibility of rain. Perhaps Pinky guessed right and my powder-blue silk blouse would not be enough to keep me warm and dry.

After an awkward moment of waiting for Pinky to say something, I said, "Dieter, do you speak English?"

With a nod, Dieter said, "Wenig Englisch."

"Florence, what did he just say?"

Not wanting to let Dieter know I understood German, I turned toward Pinky's ear and whispered, "He speaks a little English."

I smiled and said, "My name is Florence and this is Pinky."

Dieter frowned, as if to question my introduction. "Pinky?"

"Ja," I responded.

Dieter shook his head, as if to say that no German male would ever allow someone to call him by that name. Then he said, "Follow me."

He turned and started to walk away from us, across toward the upper right corner of the Hauptmarkt.

Pinky cried, "Hold on." Dieter stopped and turned back toward us.

Pinky, gripping the handle on his briefcase so tightly that his knuckles were turning white, said, "I am not moving from this spot until you tell me where we are going."

Dieter pointed toward a newsstand, "Kiosk."

I looked toward the direction Dieter had pointed. "He's taking us to a kiosk where they sell newspapers, tobacco, and all sorts of things."

Pinky shook his head. "Florence, I know what a kiosk sells. What I do not understand is why are we heading to that kiosk."

I said, "I don't know. Pinky, we'd better get a move on or we're going to lose our guide dog."

Dieter paused and waited for us until we caught up

After a few minutes of a brisk walking we reached the kiosk. That was when I noticed the white van parked next to the kiosk.

I said, Okay, Dieter, what now?"

I turned around. There were a few people walking nearby and not one of them looked like a neo-Nazi to me. By the time I turned back a second later, Dieter had vanished and was replaced by five men who had jumped out of the white van.

I didn't have time to scream for help because one of them stuffed my mouth full of cloth while another pair of hands threw a hood over my head. As I was being pushed into the van, I felt a hand rip the tracking devise from my neck and I heard it hit the ground.

I had never been attacked like that before, and the assault on the two of us was over in a few seconds. As I look back, it was obvious that these men had a plan and they knew how to execute their scheme.

About the only thing we could hope for was that Bear and Juri saw what happened and were coming to our rescue.

Chapter Twenty-Eight

Bear Zabarte—Nuremberg, Germany

As me and Juri stood in the lobby, we watched two blue dots, really Pinky and Flo, on his iPhone screen walk away from the fountain with that Dieter dude. After a minute, the two blue dots stopped moving. I ran out the lobby door, looked across the road and could just make out the three of them, Flo, Pinky, and that Dieter dude stood about half way across the big empty space. Then, they started moving away from us really fast, and I could barely tell them apart from all the other people wandering around the square.

"Juri, I don't like this. They're too far away!"

"Relax, Bear. Those tracking devices are good up to ten kilometers."

"You still got those two dots on your phone?"

"I do."

For a second, I relaxed, but I still didn't like Flo being out of sight. I glanced at Juri's phone and saw the blue dots move further away. I walked across the road just in time to see Flo and Pinky stop by a white van that was parked near a little newspaper stand.

Then, before I could do anything, a bunch of dudes jumped out of the van and stuffed my Babe and Pinky inside. "Juri, did I see that right? I know Flo has one of those tracking things around her neck so everything should be okay. But—"

"Oh my God! Bear, the two dots just disappeared."

"What the hell do you mean the dots are gone?"

Juri started to fiddle around with his phone, but I wasn't going to wait for him to fix something, not when my Babe was one of those two dots that just disappeared. I ran past the stupid fountain just as the van pulled away from the curb. The van with my Babe and the boss inside went around a corner and I could tell it was a Toyota Sienna but the license plate was too far away to pick up a number or letter.

I ran across the empty market place to where the van had been parked. On the ground by the curb, was the tracking thing that Flo had been wearing around her neck. It was crushed. Next to Flo's was the black one Pinky had put in his pocket. It was also smashed. Both tracking things looked like they'd been stomped on by some heavy boots.

I leaned over, trying to breathe, when Juri caught up to me.

I pointed to the pieces of junk on the ground. "See there…that's why the…dots… disappeared. Those bastards knew that fancy… doodad…'round Flo's neck was one of those… damn tracking things."

Juri took a bunch of big breaths, and then he said, "Did you get…close enough to see…the van's license plate?"

"No, but I saw it was a Toyota Sienna. Juri, there can't be that many white Toyota Sienna's in Nuremberg. This is Germany, damn it, not Japan."

"I'll get the local police checking on that. If it's registered in Bavaria they will find it. I will also have them put out a bulletin to be on the lookout for that vehicle." Juri kneeled down and picked up the blue pieces of Flo's tracker. "Bear, I am sorry. I was positive that nobody knew I was going to use those two tracking devices."

"Dude, somebody knew."

Chapter Twenty-Nine

Flo Sonderlund—Nuremberg, Germany

You would think that by now, with all the investigations I've done with Bear, I might have anticipated this could happen to me. I thought I knew better than to get myself into a situation like this. But one of the good things I had gained from working with Bear was that no matter what was going on around him, he never lost his cool. So that's why I'm calm even though I'm positive that once these men get their hands on Pinky's book, they'll kill us both with about as much emotion as a rock.

I'd like to think that Pinky and I survived to see Carson City again because of my superior intellect, or good looks, but if I'm honest, one of the reasons we survived was the hood the guy threw over my head had a poorly sewn seam on the right side. That allowed me to see a sliver of light between my right eye and right ear. Not much to go on but, all in all, better than nothing.

As I think back, the five men were about average height and weight, and if I had been walking toward the kiosk with Bear at my side,

I'd have given us a better than even chance of taking them out. But the guy I was with that day was Pinky, not exactly the man I'd depend on in a brawl.

Then there was one more impediment that I neglected to mention that worked against us fighting our way out, Bear or no Bear.

After the hood, and a mouthful of cloth, they tied my hands behind my back with a couple of those damn plastic ties.

Before he was gagged, I heard Pinky yell that he wouldn't let go of his briefcase. From the kidnappers limited conversation I picked up they tied his hands together, not behind his back, to the handle of his briefcase

Before the van drove off, I counted five men jump into the vehicle. The doors shut and someone drove around for ten to twenty minutes. Eventually the van stopped and I heard one say, "Hier warten, damit ich sicher sein kann, dass es sicher ist."

That told me they were waiting to be sure it was safe. While we were sitting there, I heard what sounded like the engine of a bus and then I listened to the real reason why we had a chance of surviving the kidnapping: I heard an amplified voice speaking French.

After what seemed like a long time, but was likely no more than two or three minutes, a German voice said, "Jetzt können wir sie verschieben."

If I hadn't been gagged, I could have told Pinky they said it was okay to move us.

The van moved no more than a hundred feet and then stopped again. The side door opened and a couple of hands grabbed my arms and pulled me out of the van.

I tried hard, but I still couldn't see enough through the tiny open seam to give me a hint as to where we were. As the hands pushed me forward, I felt something sharp penetrate my right arm above my elbow.

I cried a muffled, "Ouch."

"Nein sprechen."

In real pain, I pulled my arm from his grasp.

A hand grabbed my arm again, this time with a tighter grip and I heard him mumble, "Hündin," under his breath.

A mouth full of cloth kept me from screaming that I knew he had just called me a bitch, but I hoped that my understanding of the German language, and the open seam in my hood, were still the only advantages I had.

Next, I heard a loud squeak, like rusty hinges opening and old door. Then the hands pushed me into a space that felt really cold. The air smelled like damp concrete along with the hint of a toilet that hadn't been flushed for a couple of days.

A hand that smelled of beer, reached under my hood and pulled out the cloth that had been stuffed into my mouth. I could only hope that someone had done the same for Pinky.

Then the hands pushed me up against a very cold, hard wall before he walked away and once he seemed to be talking to one of the others I pulled away from the cold wall

Once I heard a bunch of footsteps walk to what sounded like another part of the cold room, I slowly turned my head to survey the room through the open seam. I could see that Pinky and I were standing against the wall in a dimly lit room. We appeared to be alone, and the sounds of voices seemed to be coming from around a corner.

I whispered, "Pinky?"

"I am standing right next to you, I think."

I took a half step to my left and bumped into him."Are you wearing a hood."

"I am, and I can't see a damn thing. Hold on, Florence, was that your hip that just bumped into me?"

"It was. Why?"

"Not sure why I asked. Just trying to get my bearings."

"Pinky, listen to me. I think they've moved to another room, because their voices are not close. Does that make any sense?"

"I agree. But why is their location so important?"

"I have a tiny opening on the right side of my hood."

"Oh my God, you can see?"

"Don't get too excited. I can't see very much."

"But I will bet that you've got a plan to get us out of here. Florence, I could kiss you."

"Bear would kill you if you did that. First I have to figure out where we are and it's going to take some time, so just stand still and don't make any noise."

Pinky whispered, "Okay. Mum's the word."

Frankly, at that point I wasn't all that sure what I was trying to do, but I was sure that a mental picture of the space had to be helpful. With my hands tied behind me, I took a tiny step back, and my hands bumped into a rough, cold wall. Next I stepped to my right, and again, and again. On the fifth step I reached the corner of what I hoped would not become our tomb.

I reversed direction, got back to Pinky and after a few more steps to my left, I reached a second corner.

I whispered, "Pinky, we're in some kind of old, concrete room. I'm going to try to get closer to the voices."

"Can you see a door or any way out of here?"

"Not yet.

"Be careful, Florence."

Suddenly Pinky Delmont, the master of hyperbole, became the king of the understatement.

"Don't worry."

I turned my head and spotted a crack of light through the little open seam. I moved along the wall, one small step at a time, as the talking got louder and the light got brighter. From the sounds of their chatter the five guys were shooting the bull and drinking beer.

Keep downing those brews guys, I thought. The more beer, the fewer brain cells I have to worry about.

Foot by foot, I slowly returned back to the corner and then to my right to where I bumped into Pinky.

"Pinky, there's a wall behind us, a wall to our right and a wall to our left. When I moved along the left wall, I could see some light and listened to the guys talking bullshit and drinking beer."

"Florence, I appreciate all that information but I still do not see how that is going to get us out of here alive."

"It will as long as they leave us alone."

"What is your plan? Are we going to sprout wings and fly back to our hotel?"

"No, I have something even better—my cell phone."

He got so excited that he nearly shouted, "Your what?"

"Pinky, keep your voice to a whisper, or my cell won't do us any good."

He whispered back. "I am sorry, Florence, you are correct."

I considered what Pinky just said, and I believe that was the first time I had ever heard him to use the word sorry toward me in any context.

"Okay, my hands are tied behind my back, but I think they bound yours in front of you. Am I correct and can you wiggle your fingers?"

"Yes, my hands are in front of me and I can wiggle my fingers."

"Great! Now the next step this is going to be awkward. I don't have any pockets in my pants, apparently designers decided women don't want pockets in their pants creating unsightly leg bulges. Anyway, I've discovered the perfect place to carry my cell phone is in my cleavage."

Pinky chuckled, "Are you kidding me?"

"No."

Pinky whispered, "How am I suppose to get to your cell phone?"

"Pinky, in case you haven't noticed, I'm positive that once the guys in the other room have finished drinking, and they've cut the ties that secure the briefcase to your hands, they'll have no reason to keep us alive. Please concentrate on extracting the cell phone, not where it is presently located."

He whispered, "Point well taken. Now, what do you want me to do?"

"You stay where you are. I'm going to lean back against the wall and slide down so you can reach inside my blouse. And don't worry about popping a button.'"

I backed up, and started to slide down the rough wall so Pinky could reach inside my bra.

It had been years since any hands, other than Bear's and my doctor's, had touched my breasts and so what I was about to ask of Pinky were the most outlandish words that had ever passed my lips.

But before I could finish considering the insanity of the moment, something very sharp, like a knife, or an ice pick, punctured the center of my back right between my shoulder blades. I moved a little left, and then right when I heard a snapping sound. It took every ounce of willpower I had to keep from screaming out in pain. I felt a trickle of warm blood run down my back. That was when I became lightheaded and my knees nearly gave way. But something inside me knew if Pinky didn't get my phone and send Bear a message, we were dead meat.

Ignoring the pain, I took a deep breath, "Now move your hands toward me."

"Florence, are you all right?"

"Not really, but we need to get this done, so shut up and stop asking stupid questions."

Had Pinky been sitting in his office at the conclusion of my comment, he would have fired me for insubordination. But we were both tied up with hoods over our heads, in a dark concrete building, under the threat of imminent death, so under those circumstances, he said, "Okay, what now."

"Move your hands toward me and when your fingers feel my blouse reach in and get my cell phone."

"Florence, that will not be easy because I have to lift the briefcase."

"I know that. Do you have a better plan?"

"Not really."

A moment later, my body gave an involuntary shiver as Pinky's freezing hands, colder than I thought they could possibly be, slipped down my cleavage.

"Florence, I have reached your phone. Now what?"

"Good. Pull it out and hold it toward me."

In the murky light that leaked through the open seam, I could see Pinky's hands wrapped around my pink iPhone.

Then it hit me that with the hood over my head, my normal facial recognition option wasn't going to unlock the phone, so I said, "I see the phone. Now swipe your finger up the screen."

"Done. Can you tell if that worked?"

"Pinky, that did it. I can see my home screen with a picture of Bear sitting in his chair holding a beer."

"Florence, I would think that you could have come up with a better picture for your home screen."

At the moment, I was pleased to see that Pinky was still his nasty old self, giving me hope that we would survive. "Now, take your finger and slide it up again."

"Done."

"Great. I can see the keypad to enter the passcode. Now key in 7856."

"How can I do that?" A touch of panic had edged into Pinky's tone. "I can't see anything."

"Don't worry, I'll watch your finger and tell you when you're hitting the right number. Now move your finger up . . . stop, now tap."

He whispered, "What did I just do?"

"You hit a seven, just three more taps to go."

Then I walked his index finger through 856. "You did it. You've unlocked my phone."

"Now what do I do?"

"Scroll up to Messages. Got it. Move your finger to the left, when you hit the side of the phone, go up. There, tap your finger. Great, you've opened up Messages."

"Now what?"

"Slide your finger up a tiny bit. There! You've opened up Bear's account. Now move your finger down to the bottom to send a text message." Pinky followed my directions. "Hold it, you're there."

"Next."

"The keyboard is a half an inch below where your finger is. Now, slowly move your finger down and I'll tell you when to stop."

Pinky whispered, "Florence, I have to set the briefcase down for a moment."

"What's wrong?"

"My finger is cramping up."

I knew we didn't have time for Pinky to rest, but as he was my only hope. And knowing what a wimp he was, I figured I couldn't push him too fast. "Okay, rest for a minute."

I silently counted to thirty. "Okay, Pinky, your minute is up."

"That seemed very quick." He lifted his briefcase, hand, and finger back to message.

I said, "Now, move your finger down about and I'll tell you when to stop."

Pinky did as instructed and I whispered, "Perfect. Now tap your finger."

I almost burst into tears when I saw the z in the text box. "That was great. Now, move your finger up one space and to the right two spaces."

Pinky, in a harsh whisper, demanded, "Slow down, Florence. With my hands bound up like this, and the weight of the briefcase typing does not come easy."

"Got it. Your finger is over the f so tap."

A zf now populated the message field.

"Okay, slide your finger down two spaces. Spot on. Tap. Now slide two spaces to the left."

"Am I in the right spot?"

"A little further left. Now you are there. Tap."

"Florence, are we almost finished? My hand is starting to cramp up again. I cannot continue this much longer."

"I understand." But truthfully, I didn't understand. I figured the real blood running down my back trumped a little cramping of his fingers. "Hang in there, we're almost done. Okay, slide your finger up three spaces, slow down, a little further. Stop! Now tap on the 3.

Move your finger one space to the right and tap on the 4. Great."

"Florence, I have to set the briefcase down again to see if I can clear the cramp from my index finger."

"Pinky, there are just a few taps to go. You can do this."

"Not right now. Maybe in five minutes after I let my hand and fingers rest."

"I'm afraid we don't have that much time. Anytime now those guys are going to remember they've got to do something with the two people they've kidnapped."

"I know that, but I cannot control my cramped finger."

I feared that zf 34 might not be enough of a clue, but it was obvious that Pinky wasn't going to budge. I said, "Okay, we'll go with the zf 34. All you have to do is tap the up arrow to send."

"I will see if I can use my little finger."

Once the message was sent, the thrill of success temporarily masked my pain, but then the adrenaline wore off and the spot between my shoulders began to throb again."

Pinky said, "Now what do we do?"

"I'll slide down the wall again so you can put the phone back where it was stored. And Pinky, it's our little secret about where I keep my phone and that secret will remain between us. Got it?"

"I understand your concern. Your secret will remain safe with me."

As I moved down the wall, whatever had punctured me was lodged in my back and hurt me more as I slid down. Then, I felt Pinky's icy fingers slip my phone back into my cleavage.

"Florence, I think I have accomplished that task. Does the phone feel secure?"

With the shooting pain in my back and tears streaming down my face, I didn't immediately respond.

"Florence, I cannot see anything so I am completely dependent on your vocal response. Please answer me."

I took a big breath to hope the pain would subside. "Yes, Pinky, you did a great job. I'm sorry, but when I leaned against the wall the first time, something sharp dug into my back. I hope that I'm not bleeding too much."

"Do you feel strong enough to answer a few questions?"

"I think so."

"What does zf stand for?"

"Zeppelin Field."

"And you think that is where we are presently imprisoned?"

"I do."

"And why are you so sure that is where we are incarcerated?"

"When we first arrived, I heard a bus drive by with and a guide was speaking French. I'm sure that we are at Zeppelin Field because a French speaking tourist bus drove by us when Juri was showing us around Zeppelin Field."

"Florence, there must be tourist buses like that all over Nuremberg. I'd get thrown out of court for providing such scant evidence."

"Right or wrong, I'm staking our lives on that scant evidence.

Pinky was silent for a moment, then he said, "What about the 34?"

"Zeppelin Field is ringed with 34 concrete buildings and I'm positive we are inside one of those buildings."

"Once again. Your evidence seems very limited."

"Pinky, did notice the faint order of urine?"

"I did, but–"

"Juri told us that the 34 concrete buildings next to Zeppelin Field served as public bathrooms during the Nazi rallies."

"But that was over fifty years ago!"

"I know you can't see, but can you feel how cold and dank it is in here. The concrete in these buildings could easily hold onto smells for centuries."

"Alright. So you think we are in one of those 34 buildings?

"I do."

"Now that I understand your rational behind the zf34. But do you think Bear will get the code?"

I hesitated. A wave of nausea hit me when the thing in my back seemed to hit a nerve. "I'm sure he will."

"Florence, one final question. Do you think we'll be rescued?"

"Yes, Pinky. We will be rescued."

What I didn't tell him was that I wasn't really sure, but at that point I was freezing, in pain, and bleeding, so to tell the truth, I didn't care one way or another.

Chapter Thirty

Bear Zabarte—Nuremberg, Germany

I was staring out the window of the same hotel room that my Babe left more than an hour ago. Juri was screaming into his phone, when my cell chirped. I pulled it out of my back pocket and there was a text from Flo.

"Jesus, I just got a text from my Babe. Maybe she and Pinky got away?"

I opened up Messages to read the text, but it didn't make any sense to me. Just two letters and two numbers.

"Juri, what the hell does zf34 mean?"

Juri stopped yelling into his phone and said, "Did they get away?"

I held my phone screen in front of Juri's face. "You tell me. I don't get it."

He glanced at my screen, and then went back to yelling at his phone, like it was more important to get the local cops looking for the white Toyota van.

I ripped Juri's phone out of his hand and stuck my phone screen damn near into his eyes, so the screen was the only thing the dude could see. Then, like a light bulb had just turned on, he grabbed my phone and cried, "I think I know where they are. Let's go."

We ran out my hotel room door and down the stairs 'cause we didn't have time to wait for the elevator. We had to save my Babe and the boss.

When we hit the street I yelled, "Juri, slow down and tell me where the hell we're going."

He didn't answer me until we were in his car and racing down a street with the siren wailing.

"I'm pretty sure the zf stands for Zeppelin Field. 34 for one of the 34 concrete buildings that provide the backdrop to the field."

"I remember that place now. You told us some dude built those buildings so the troops could take a dump. You told us they were used also to hold up those giant Nazi flags so Hitler could stand where we stood and see all…Jeeze, I'll betcha you're right, Juri, my Babe and Pinky are stuck in one of those damn buildings."

"Bear, once we get closer to Zeppelin Field I'm going to shut down the siren because I don't want to warn the kidnappers that the cops are on the way."

"Good idea. How far now?"

"About five K's."

"What the hell is a K?"

249

"I am sorry. K is short for kilometer, the equivalent of about six tenths of one of your miles. That means we are about three miles from Zeppelin Field."

"Okay, just step on it."

While Juri raced through the streets of Nuremberg, I thought about Juri's chicken-shit informant dude who took my Babe and Pinky to the van and set them up for the kidnappers.

"Juri, I don't know what sorta things you go through here in Germany when you recruit an informant, but you need to work on some of those things."

"Bear, I imagine the process to recruit a confidential informant in Germany is about the same as in your country. I knew that Dieter was a marginal character, but at the time he was my only way to get to the neo-Nazis."

"I probably shouldn't be telling you this, you being a cop an all, but that Dieter guy is a dead man walking if anything happens to my Babe."

"Bear, I am sure you realize that I cannot, and will not, allow you to kill Dieter, but I do understand how you feel."

As Juri played dodgeball with the Nuremberg afternoon traffic, I thought about what he just told me: that if I killed Dieter, he would throw me in the slam. But, if I was gonna spend the rest of my life without my

Babe, I might as well do it in a German prison knowing that the dude who set her up was pushing up daisies.

About a minute of no talking passed between us when Juri said, "I am going to shut down the siren as we are nearly at Zeppelin Field."

I said, "You got any idea which one of those 34 toilets Flo might be in?"

"Not really. Assuming the message from Flo is correct, the kidnappers had to cut through a chain-link fence the city placed to block the public from entering the buildings. I will start at the north end of the buildings, drive by each one until we find the one with a cut chain-link fence."

"Juri, what the hell do we do if we don't find a cut in the chain-link fence?"

"Bear, I'm sure that Flo and Pinky are being held in one of those buildings. We are dealing with a gang of neo-Nazis. The Zeppelin Field is hallowed ground to those bastards."

For the first time since I saw Pinky and Flo get kidnapped, I relaxed. "Juri, that's something we agree on. Those new-Nazis are bastards!"

Chapter Thirty-One

Flo Sonderlund—Nuremberg, Germany

A loud creak from a rusty door hinge startled me. Someone entered and while I listened to footsteps, I turned my head slightly in a futile attempt to see if I could tie a face to the steps. The footsteps paused, as if that person wanted to look us over, and then the steps continued on to join the others.

Pinky whispered, "Did you see who that was?"

The shooting pain in my back had settled down to a dull throb. "No. Be quiet. I need to hear what they are saying to help us get out of here."

But had I been totally honest with Pinky, the only advantage I had understanding German was that I would know when and how they were going to kill us. My depressing thoughts were interrupted when I heard multiple voices cry out, "Sieg heil, mein Führer!"

That was followed by a single male voice that responded with, "Heil."

Pinky whispered, "Do you know what they are saying?"

I snapped back, "I might be able to figure that out if you'd keep quiet."

"Sorry."

I don't know why but I closed my eyes when I had that stupid hood over my head, but it was as if I felt like I could better focus my sense of hearing with my eyes shut.

The voice that had responded 'Heil' to the 'Sieg heil, mein Führer' was obviously the leader of the pack. He scolded them for making a mess and told them to clean up the area.

"Pinky, the five men that kidnapped us called the man who just came in their Führer which means leader. He told them to stop drinking beer and to clean up the mess."

After I listened to some rummaging around and the cascading sound of breaking glass, I heard him ask if they had the book yet. A voice told him they were waiting for his instructions.

Pinky whispered, "Florence, I am positive I have heard that voice before. I just cannot be sure where."

"Quiet, he's telling them to do something with us."

"Florence, what did he say?" Pinky whispered after a moment.

I was searching for a gentle way to tell my boss he was about to have both his hands chopped off when something crashed against the metal door.

Chapter Thirty-Two

Bear Zabarte—Nuremberg, Germany

Juri yelled, "There is the first one of the thirty-four buildings."

A half-a-block away I spotted the first concrete crapper.

Juri, flipped a switch on his phone and said, "From this point on, I am recording the rest of our investigation."

Then he started talking like one of those dudes who speak to tourists on a bus."I am turning right on to Hermann-Bohm Strasse. The first building is on my left and the chain-link fence looks solid…and the second…"

Juri went on like that until he slammed on the brakes by the tenth building. The chain-link fence was cut wide open and parked under a big tree was a white van.

Before Juri took his foot off the brake, I jumped out of the car. I ran to the rusty door and just before I hit the old metal, Juri yelled, "Bear, be careful. There's an Audi parked behind the van."

Shit, I didn't care if there was a fleet of Audi's parked next to the white van. All I knew was I had to get into that old German john before my Babe got hurt.

I hit the door with my full weight and the damn thing popped open easier than I thought. As I almost fell into the room, I couldn't see a thing 'cause the only light was coming from the sunlight behind me.

I yelled, "Babe, are you in here?"

On my left I heard her say, "Bear! Thank God you're here." Then, after a little sob, "I told Pinky that the cavalry would arrive in time."

But before I could move toward my Babe, a bunch of young dudes rushed into the room between me and Flo. I bashed three of them and had just grabbed the next one when behind me Juri yelled, "Polizei! Hände in der Luft oder ich werde schießen."

I was holding a German kidnapper a good six inches off the ground and was about to smash him one in the face, when he raised his hands, like he wanted to surrender. So did the last guy who was crawling around my feet on his hands and knees like a dog who couldn't figure out how to get away.

I dropped the dude and turned to my left. Through the dark, I could see Flo and the boss were standing about ten feet away tucked in a corner. They both had hoods on their heads and Pinky's hood was shaking like he was freezing or something.

I ran over and lifted the hood off my Babe's head. She kinda squeaked as I gave her a little kiss. Then Flo flashed me a brave smile and said, "I'm glad you didn't hug me because my back's a little sore, and my hands are tied behind my back with plastic ties. Do you have something that can cut the damned plastic?"

I lifted off Pinky's hood, and pulled out my pocket knife, but before I could cut the plastic ties off Flo and Pinky, a voice I kinda recognized came from the back area behind me.

"Juri, als Ihr unmittelbarer Vorgesetzter gebe ich Ihnen einen direkten Befehl, Ihre Waffe fallen zu lassen, oder ich werde gezwungen sein, die drei Amerikaner zu erschießen."

I whispered, "Babe, what the hell did that dude just say?"

"Something along the line of, 'Juri, as your immediate supervisor, I give you a direct order to drop your weapon or I will be forced to shoot the three Americans.'"

As his words sunk in, Detective Bauman, the same German cop me and Flo met at the airport, walked out of the dark and into the stream of sunlight coming through the open door. In Bauman's hand was one of those old German Lugers that looked like it was straight out of an old World War II movie.

I glanced back at Juri. In his right hand he held a 9mm Glock, a standard cop pistol. And if I had to make a bet, his Glock was loaded with hollow points. So my money in this little standoff was on Juri.

I said, "Bauman, or Hitler, or whatever these five new-Nazi piss-ants call you, you go right ahead and pull the trigger. You might get me, but you'll never get all three of us 'cause about the time you get that second shot off, Juri's Glock will blow you in half. Now, if you were packing an Uzi instead of that tired old Luger, I'd give you an even chance to get all of us, but you aren't holding an Uzi. How about you set that old Luger down? Who knows, if you get a really good lawyer, like Pinky, you might get out of the slam in time to see your great-grandkids graduate from high school."

With the barrel of that Luger pointed straight at my forehead, it seemed to me that time sorta froze in the cold, smelly room.

Later, my Babe told me that from her perspective, nobody moved for about ten seconds, and we made up a perfect tableau.

Don't ask me what a tablow is, or how to spell it, but that was the word she used. Anyway, here's what it looked like to me—the three dudes I had cold-cocked were lying on the floor—the forth guy I was about to send to happy-land was sitting on the floor crying—the

258

fifth dude was still on all fours—me, Flo, Pinky, Juri, and the new-Hitler, were sorta frozen in place. About all that seemed to be missing from Flo's tablow was a table with four dogs playing poker.

Suddenly, the new-Hitler spun around and disappeared into the dark. Before me or Juri could move, a single shot rang out. I figured that the new-Hitler went out just like the old Hitler. Both were yellow-bellied bastards who were too chicken to face the music.

While I cut the plastic ties off Flo and Pinky's hands, Juri put plastic ties on the five kidnappers and attached all of them to a solid pipe that ran down the wall behind Pinky.

I said, "How you doing, boss?"

"I know that I have never been happier to see you. My boy, you have a job for life as my chief investigator, even if you do call me boss."

Flo said, "Does that include me?"

"Of course, Florence. Without you, your courage, your phone, and your clever code, Bear and Juri would have never found us."

Flo nodded. "And I imagine that by now we'd both be dead. So in the future, I'm sure you'll agree to one little stipulation for any of our future investigations."

"And what is that stipulation, Florence?"

"No more Coach flights. We will fly Business class wherever our investigations take us with no arguments from you."

Pinky gave a little sigh, "Florence, Business class for you and Bear is a small price to pay for my life. I agree to your stipulation."

Juri said, "Bear, I think we had better go back and check out Bauman, just to make sure he's dead."

We walked around the dark corner and Juri pulled out his flashlight. As he clicked it on we saw Bauman's body slumped against a wall. The top half of his head and most of his brains were splattered across the concrete.

I shook my head. "Don't worry, Juri, the dude's dead. Seeing what's left of his head, I might have been wrong about the fire power of that old Luger."

He laughed, "Not really. When someone sticks the barrel of a gun to the roof of his mouth, barrel up, and then pulls the trigger, even an old Luger is capable of doing quite a bit of damage."

Tired of looking at the dead Nazi, I said, "Juri, shine that light around the area."

The corner near Bauman's body was littered with empty beer bottles.

I said, "These dudes couldn't have been here for much more than an hour. They sure knew how to throw down the beer."

Juri nodded, then he moved his light up, onto the wall above the body. Hanging there was a bright red flag and in the middle was one of those Nazi signs. Above the flag was some spray-painted words, but I couldn't read 'em 'cause they was written in German.

"Juri, can you translate that for me?"

I watched his eyes move along the words and he nodded. "In English it says, 'The Party is Hitler and Hitler is Germany just as Germany is Hitler!—Rudolf Hess.'"

"Was he one of Hitler's buds?"

"He was more than a buddy. In 1938, Hess was appointed Deputy Führer to Hitler. Then in1941, early in the war, Hess stole a plane and flew to Scotland in a strange, and some say crazy attempt to negotiate peace with England. The Brits kept him in custody until the end of the war when Hess was returned to Germany to stand trial here in Nuremberg as one of the major war criminals. The Court convicted him of crimes against peace and of conspiracy with other German leaders to commit crimes. He escaped execution and was given a life sentence in Spandau Prison where he died 1987 at the age of 93. The official word is that Hess hanged himself with a lamp cord, but a second autopsy said the marks on his neck were consistent with strangulation, not hanging."

I said, "That's a hell of a story."

"I agree, but there is more. Once Hess died, Spandau prison was demolished and the government went to the extent of grinding up all the rocks and bricks into sand to prevent the prison from becoming a neo-Nazi shrine. The final punch line to the story happened in 1990 when a shopping center to serve the British military community in Germany was built on the old prison grounds."

I said, "Looks like the Brits finally got their way with the Nazis.

As I turned to go back to Flo, I took one last glance at Bauman's body and shuddered as I realized that could have been me lying on the cold, concrete floor.

I smiled at Flo, then walked up to the five Nazi pissants that Juri had tied to a pipe.

"Juri, before Bauman interrupted me, I managed to punch three of these little bastards for what they did to my Babe. I know what I'm gonna ask ain't legit, but I didn't get the chance to smash the other two in the face and that really ain't right. Can you do me a favor and close your eyes for a couple of seconds?"

He nodded.

While the two Nazi bastards tried to squirm away, I grabbed each one behind his head and bashed him a solid one on the nose.

"Okay, Juri. You can open your eyes now."

He opened them and chuckled, "Oh my goodness, two of my prisoners have suddenly developed nose bleeds. I wonder how that happened?"

"Juri, I owe you one for letting me do that. After we get Flo and Pinky back to our hotel, me and you need to head back to that beer joint so I can buy you a couple of rounds."

More then ready to get the hell out of this shit hole, I walked back to where I'd left Flo. When I gave her a little hug she cried out. In all the excitement, I forgot she told me her back hurt a little. "Babe, move over into the light so I can see what's wrong with your back."

There was a small tear and and some blood down the back of her favorite blue shirt When I looked real close, through the tear, I spotted what looked like a piece of rusty wire sticking out of her skin.

I didn't say anything but that hunk of rusty wire really creeped me out. I didn't know how much was still stuck in her, or how much damage it had done, or might still do.

"Babe, you're still bleeding a little and I wanna see why."

I turned her away from the eager eyes and lifted the back of her shirt up a little. Just above her bra, I could see the end of the wire and how much she was bleeding. Hell, I know I'm not a doctor, but that wire didn't look good.

The blood wasn't gushing out, but there was more coming out than I thought there should be. And that damn rusty wire was fat! About as big around as an old wire coat hanger.

I didn't want to scare her, so I lied a little. "Babe, it looks like the bleeding's almost stopped now." Then, keeping my voice nice and calm, I said, "Juri, on the way to our hotel, we need to stop by a doc to get Flo's back checked out. Just to be sure she's okay."

"Right. We'll do that as soon as my colleagues arrive so they can arrest the five suspects."

I took another look at my Babe's back, and then at the five piss-ants attached to the pipe with plastic ties. "Juri, those bastards aren't going anywhere. We need to go now."

Juri walked over to me and I pulled my fingers across my lips, like zip up your pie hole.

Looking at the blood on Flo's back, he nodded. "Good idea. Let's go."

It took us a few minutes to get Flo and Pinky settled inside Juri's car. I held the front door open for Pinky, then I helped Flo into the back seat. Taking her hand I said, "Babe, I won't belt you in 'cause I know you don't want to get any blood on the back seat of Juri's car. I'll put my belt on and hold on to you incase Juri's has to hit the brakes hard. Got it, Juri."

I saw Juri nod, like he understood we needed to get Flo to the doc's as fast as he could without dumping her onto the floor.

My arm around my wounded Babe, Juri backed his car onto the road. I glanced back at the concrete building that the Nazi dude had built for Hitler. Then it hit me. Until Juri told me about these new-Nazis in Germany, I'd been living in my own stupid dream world, and I can't be the only dumb American. Shit, as a graduate of Elko High, I'm pretty smart. And Pinky sent me and Flo all over he world to do his investigations. I've traveled to places like California, North Carolina, Hawaii, Denmark, Sweden, even China. But in all the places me and Flo have ever been, and all the murderers we'd caught, we'd never run across evil bastards like these German new-Nazis. I mean these Nazis are ten times worse than the baddest dudes we'd caught before now.

Flo squeezed my hand.

"How you doing Babe?"

"Bear, I can almost hear the gears grinding in your head. What's going on in there?"

"It's these new-Nazis."

She said, "Actually, I think they're called neo-Nazis, not new-Nazis."

I said, "Whatever. Juri told us that the new-Nazis wanted to take over the world again, just like that chicken shit Hitler tried to do, and I just figured out that we can't let that happen. I know some dudes that barf up all kinds of hate talk back in Carson City, but they're not called new-Nazis, they're called white supremacists. From now on, when I hear anybody spew that sort of crap, I'm gonna give him two choices: shut up, or get up close and personal with my right fist!"

Flo smiled. "I had a feeling that you'd come up with a simple solution to solve the world's neo-Nazi problem."

"Babe, my mom, one of the nicest people in the world, would say that the new-Nazis in Germany, and America's white supremacists, were all cut from the same bolt of cloth. But like I said, my mom was a really nice lady who never used bad words. I'd say they all crawled out of the same pot of shit. What do you think, Babe?"

When she didn't answer, I glanced at her and noticed that she looked really pale.

"Like I said, what do you think?"

"Bear, I'm not thinking straight. I'm a little dizzy. I guess it's all the excitement. I need to get back to the hotel so I..." Her head suddenly dropped to her chest.

I yelled, "Juri, my Babe just passed out. You need to find a hospital, pronto."

Chapter Thirty-Three

Bear Zabarte—Nuremberg, Germany

Juri drove like a bat out of hell. In fact, he drove so fast that it scared me a little, but I was glad 'cause we got Flo to a hospital fast.

Juri pulled up in front of the hospital, slammed on the brakes, and bolted out of the car before I could say anything. One of the good parts of having Juri with us was it cut down all that "I don't speak German" crap.

The next thing I saw was three nurses pushing one of those hospital beds on wheels to Juri's car. Two of them helped me lift Flo out and laid her down on her side and pushed her bed into the hospital. I followed the nurses and Flo down a hall.

Juri said to one of the nurses, "Sie sprechen kein Deutsch. Er ist ihr Mann. Ich warte draußen."

I asked, "Hey what'd you just say to her?"

"You do not speak German. You are her husband. And I will be back after I drive Pinky to the hotel."

Then Juri turned and left the hospital.

Before you get your skivvies twisted into a knot, I know me and Flo ain't married, but my Babe could be in trouble and I wasn't going to let nobody do nothing to her without me being there.

The nurse gave me the high sign so I followed her as she pushed Flo into what I figured was kinda an emergency room. The nurse wheeled Flo to a bed. A couple of big dudes walked up, counted out loud with what almost sounded one, two, three, and just like that Flo was laying on a real bed.

I guess I was standing to close 'cause the nurse took my arm and pulled me away from the bed as a doc came in. He stuck his hand out, "I am Doctor Schmidt and you are Mr.?"

"Bear Zabarte."

"And this is Mrs. Zabarte?"

"Not really. We live together and—"

The doc snapped, "Mr. Zabarte, I am sorry, but as you are not her husband, we cannot allow you to remain in the Emergency Room. Please go to the waiting room and I will contact you with any information that I am allowed to give to a non-family member."

"But, she's—"

Before I could get out my next word, the same two big dudes that helped lift Flo onto her bed grabbed me and they actually carried me down the hall into a waiting room.

So just 'cause some stupid real husband rule, I was stuck by myself in the waiting room until Juri showed up.

I said, "How's Pinky doing?"

"He did not speak to me, I think he was still in a state of shock. I was afraid to leave him alone in his hotel room, so I called for a support backup. That is what took me so long."

So me and Juri hung out in this little room with a couple of chairs and a pile of old German newspapers for what seemed like forever. But Juri told me later it was only an hour.

I couldn't just sit on my ass and wait, not with my Babe hurting so bad, so I walked around, and around, and around, that stupid room. I was ready to storm back to where Flo was, even if I had to fight my way in, when that hard ass Doc Schmidt waltzed in to the waiting room.

"Herr Zabarte, Frau Florence has given me permission to inform you that she is much improved. Somehow her back became impaled on a thick wire. Using your American measurement system, I would guess the wire was a little more than six inches long. Her injury was caused by a wire that broke off from some heavy metal mesh that is used in construction projects to enhance the strength of the concrete walls. There were two major problems with Frau Florence's injury. First, and most important, was her loss of blood. We infused her with two units of her blood type and that action removed the immediate threat to her life. Then we were faced with extracting the wire from her back. An X-ray indicated the wire was a few millimeters from puncturing her spinal column, but the emergency surgeon was able remove the wire with no damage. One final item, the wire was old and rusty. Do you happen to know where it came from?"

"Yup. Flo told me it broke off a concrete wall inside one of Hitler's thirty-four shit houses."

The doc stared at me, like his English maybe wasn't as good as he thought it was. So Juri jumped up and fired off a whole bunch of German words to the doc. I don't have a clue what Juri told him, but at one point the doc nodded, and then he shook his head. The doc turned to me, and said, "Mr. Zabarte, I apologize that you were exposed to the neo-Nazi and criminal underbelly of my city, Nuremberg. Because the rusty wire punctured her skin we have given her a tetanus shot. Also, considering the origin of the wire, I will give you a small bottle with 16 capsules that contain a powerful antibiotic. Please make sure Frau Florence takes all the pills in the container, so she will be able to fight off all the potential bacteria that she could have come into contact inside that 75 year-old, public toilet."

I said, "Thanks, doc."

"Mr. Zabarte. You are welcome, and I want to apologizing to you. Frau Florence explained to me that you are like husband and wife. Please go and visit with your Frau."

I ran down the hall, and rushed into the Emergency Room. Even ten feet from her bed I could tell that the doc had done a really great job. Real color had come back to my Babe's face.

I smiled and she smiled back. "Babe, you look like a million bucks."

"So do you."

"How do you feel?"

"I'm okay. My back's still a little tender, but nowhere near as bad as it felt when you brought me in here. The doctor didn't tell me much about what had punctured my back. Did he tell you?"

"Yup. It was about a six-inch long, rusty piece of the steel mesh the Nazis used to reinforce the concrete walls when they built those 34 shit houses."

"That sounds pretty nasty. How deep did it go?"

"Babe, it was really close to your back bone. That's why they had to bring a special doc to get it out."

"So I'm good now?"

"Sorta. Because that room you and Pinky were thrown into used to be an old toilet, the doc wants you to take the pills he gave me. I've got 'em in my pocket in a little bottle."

"I can do that. Can we go back to the hotel now?"

"We can, and the doc told me that if you feel up to it, we can fly home the day after tomorrow.

"Make the reservations. After a couple of days rest, I'll be ready to head home."

Chapter Thirty-Four

Bear Zabarte—Nuremberg, Germany

I got Flo back to the hotel and after I made sure she was all tucked in bed I told her, "If it's okay with you, I'm gonna check on Pinky, and after that, hit that beer joint with Juri 'cause we owe him big. Babe, I don't want to think about what would have happened if Juri hadn't figured out what the hell zf 34 meant. I know Juri's a cop, but he's one of the good ones, so we owe him a couple of brews."

My Babe rolled over, pulled the pillow around her head, and said, "Sounds good to me. Oh, don't forget to bring home the receipts. I'm sure Pinky will agree that this is a legitimate business expense. I'll just catch a little shuteye while you're gone."

I stood there for a second and thought about how close I had come to losing her. I gave Flo a little kiss on her forehead. She wiggled a little, and went back to snoring.

I tiptoed out of our room and headed to Pinky's

After damn near pounding on his door, he opened it a crack and peeked out.

"Bear, I was attempting to fall asleep. What has come up that demands my immediate attention?"

Jesus, he can still come up with ways to piss me off. "Boss, I just put Flo to bed so she can recover from the hole in her back. Actually I stopped by to make sure you're okay, but after what you just said, I guess I really don't give a shit."

I turned and started to walk away when Pinky squeaked, "Bear, I apologize. Please come in and sit down."

Pinky's really good at that. He can go from being a nasty bastard to a nice guy faster than a top fry cook can flip a pancake.

"Okay, but just for a minute. I promised to buy Juri a beer. So, how are you doing?"

"Physically, except for abrasions and bruises on my wrists, I am okay."

He walked around the room for a couple of seconds, like somebody was chasing him. I could see that something bad was bugging him, but before I could ask him what it was, he started talking again.

"Every time I close my eyes, I am back in that cold room with a hood over my head. I can smell the damp concrete, I can hear our kidnappers talking about us, but I don't know what they are saying. I can't shake the feeling that something horrific was about to happen to me when you and Juri rescued me."

"Boss, we didn't just rescue you. We got Flo too, and took care of those Nazis bastards."

"I know that, but that tiny bit of knowledge does not reduce my fear of closing my eyes."

I think my Babe would tell Pinky that he wasn't the only one hurting, but Flo was snoozing. I said, "So when you want to take an afternoon nap, like right now, you're afraid to close your eyes 'cause you keep feeling like you're still inside that old shit house, right?"

"That could be one way of describing my difficulty."

"Boss. What do you think happens when me and Flo are out there doing your dirty work? Hell, I've been shot more than once. Nearly drowned. One time, a broad tried to slice me in half with a meat cleaver. And remember that Vegas mob boss who sent his dudes out to get me. That sort of dangerous shit happens to me and Flo damn near every time we take off on one of your investigations. To me, it just comes with the job."

Pinky stood there for a second and stared at me. "Bear, are you telling me that you can't sleep because you keep seeing and hearing things from past investigations?"

"Nope. Once I crawl into the sack, I sleep like a baby. What I'm trying to tell you is that when you normally go to work, you sit behind a desk in your office, or you're in a courtroom, and you're safe."

"My boy, I do not think—"

"Hey, it's my turn to talk. Me and Flo don't have a safe office or courtroom like you do. When you send us on an assignment, we both know that sooner or later some shit's gonna hit the fan and so far, we've been pretty good at making sure none of that stuff gets on us. One time, after a really close call, Flo told me that the danger comes with the territory. I don't know what the hell territory has got to do with anything, but that's what she said."

As Pinky started to push me toward his door, he said, "I guess I never thought about how much your lives were in danger during those assignments."

"It's about time you do. Hey, you're alive, and still have that damned book that got all of us into this mess."

"My goodness, with everything else going on, I almost forgot about the book."

"Boss, you gonna try to sell it here in kraut land?"

He looked up at the ceiling, like the answer was written up there. "No. I will take it back home where I have a known buyer."

"You talking about the same guy you were suppose to meet with Hook in Vegas?"

"Yes, that is my plan."

"The same dude that scared you so much that you dumped Hook and hopped on a plane to Germany?"

"The same man, except this time I will have you, my trusted bodyguard by my side."

Oh shit! "Boss, I'm good, but I'm only one dude. Those Vegas mob guys are tough and there's a whole bunch of them."

"I have complete faith in you, my boy. Now, if you will excuse me, I am due to take a little nap."

Pinky shoved me out of his room and quickly shut the door. While riding down the elevator, I called Juri to tell him I was on my way to the beer hall.

I was on my second brew when Juri walked in. He stopped by the bar and the babe with a great rack poured him a beer. I noticed he didn't look too happy as he headed to my table.

I jumped up, "Hi, Juri, how's it hanging?"

"Bear, I am never quite sure how to answer that question." He looked around, like he wanted to make sure nobody could hear him. "Are you referring to that part of a male's anatomy that hangs between his legs?"

"Yup."

He frowned. "Then I guess I am hanging as good as one could expect."

"Was there a big hullaballoo at the office when the word got out about your boss doing the Lugar mouthwash?"

"Not as much as one would expect. I have had suspicions about Bauman's Neo-Nazi involvement for some time. But, as he was my superior, I kept my concerns to myself."

I lifted my beer mug.

Juri lifted his.

We clinked and downed a big swig.

"Juri, my dealings with cops haven't been too great, but I've got to say that you're one of the good ones."

"Thank you, Bear. Working with you and Flo has given me a fresh view of Americans."

We emptied our mugs. I got up, walked to the bar, set them down and said, "Savvy beers."

She frowned, like she didn't understand my German. Then she held up two fingers. I nodded and in a few seconds I was back sitting with Juri.

We did that clinking thing again, downed a mouthful, and then Juri said, "The one spot I did not take you and Flo to is the location where the Nuremberg trials took place."

"Hey, I remember that movie. I saw it a long time ago."

"I am not talking about the movie. This is the real thing. After this beer, I will drive you by."

"Is there something interesting to look at, like we saw at that Zeppelin Field?"

Juri sat back and kinda scrunched up his face. "Now that you mention it the old Palace of Justice does look like many other buildings in Nuremberg."

"Great, so we don't have to go. How about you tell me about the trial while we down a few more brews."

"Good idea."

Juri was my kind of stand up dude.

He took a big gulp, and said, "As Nuremberg was considered the birthplace of the Nazi party, my city was chosen as the fitting place to mark the Nazis symbolic demise. The Palace of Justice had some courtrooms and a large prison was also part of the complex. Twenty-four major war criminals were tried during the first trial that started on November 20, 1945. It took almost a year to reach the verdicts where all but three of the defendants were found to be guilty. Twelve were sentenced to death, one in absentia, and the other twelve were given prison sentences ranging from 10 years to life behind bars. Ten of the condemned were executed by hanging on October 16, 1946, fifteen days after the trial ended. The eleventh, Hermann Göring, committed suicide the night before his execution."

"That's about what I recall from the movie. Juri, are you ready for another beer?"

He started to reach for his wallet. "It is my turn to buy this round."

"Nope, I've got it."

This time I didn't even have to ask for savvy beers. The babe behind the bar had poured two fresh ones by the time I got there.

After my butt hit the seat and I took a swig of my beer, I said, "As soon as I get back to the hotel, I'm gonna make reservations to fly us back home."

Juri started to say something, stopped, took a big swig of beer and then he said, "You may not know the answer to this question, but is Pinky planning on taking the Achtliederbuch back to America?"

"I'm pretty sure that's what he's gonna do. Why?"

"I would love to come up with a legal reason to stop him, but I cannot think of one at the moment. Bear, that first edition of Luther's hymnal is more than a book, it is important to Germany's history, and as such, the Achtliederbuch means much more to my nation than money."

"I've gotcha, but my boss is Pinky, and he collects money like some people collect stamps. I'll try to talk him into giving the book to you Germans, where it belongs, but if I were you, I wouldn't hold my breath."

"Thank you, Bear. Now, I am positive it is my turn to buy the last round."

Chapter Thirty-Five

Flo Sonderlund—Somewhere high over the State of Kansas

As usually happens when Bear and I fly anywhere, I've been given the task of bringing you up to date.

After a quick puddle jumper flight from Nuremberg to Munich, we boarded a Lufthansa Airbus 350 for an eleven-and-a-half-hour flight from Munich to San Francisco, and then another puddle jumper to Reno.

It's a little hard for me to believe that three days ago, Pinky and I had been kidnapped and were being held against our will inside one of the thirty-four Nazi concrete buildings that surrounded the Zeppelin Field.

Since I had teamed up with Bear, during our many investigations to clear one of Pinky's clients, I had experienced some danger. But I have never feared for my life like I had during my captivity when Pinky and I were both hooded and hog-tied like two people on their way to be slaughtered.

Even now, when I close my eyes, I can still sense the rough, cold, damp walls with my fingertips as I felt my way around our concrete prison. I can still smell the lingering tang of a public toilet. My heart still pounds as I wait for Pinky's scream when the kidnappers saw off his hands. Finally, the ultimate terror when Bauman coldly stated that he was going to shoot all of the Americans pointing his pistol directly at us.

Presently, as I sit warm and in my comfortable Business class seat, I know this will sound a little crazy, but I still feel vulnerable.

In fact, every time I closed my eyes, even on this plane, I found it was impossible to completely escape from my mental images of horror. I made a silent pledge with myself to seek out a local shrink who could help me get past my Nuremberg nightmares when we get back to Carson City.

My thoughts of Nuremberg were interrupted when I noticed a flight attendant push a cart filled with drinks next to Pinky who was sitting in first class, just in front of business class. I had been entertained throughout the flight by Pinky's futile attempts to arrange a later rendezvous with the young attendant. Frankly, part of me was pleased to see that Pinky had returned to his old self—the man who was in love with love—while the other part of me had hoped that our terrifying experience in Nuremberg had somehow changed Pinky for the better.

Bear, who was in the seat next to me was as usual sawing logs.

This flight was no different than the rest. Bear had a true fear of flying, but he felt that a grown man should never show fear, so he'd down three or four beers, a couple of melatonin, yawn and fall asleep.

As long as my man was happy, I didn't care how many beers he drank. By sleeping through ninety percent of a flight, he was a happy camper, and that meant we were both happy campers.

In fact, I'll never forget the feeling of absolute joy I experienced when he rushed into my concrete prison to rescue me. Today, as I looked at his peaceful face, I made myself a second pact. I didn't know how or when, but this was the man I wanted to spend the rest of my life with. All I had to do was figure out a way to pop the question.

As I leaned to my right, to get an updated picture of Pinky's progress with the attendant, I felt a slight pain shoot down the center of my back, reminding me of my close call with paralysis. The emergency room doctor told me that the heavy wire he had extracted had come very close to severing some nerves in my spinal column, potentially paralyzing a limb or two. I told him that he should not pass on that prognosis to Bear and he agreed.

I watched the cart move toward my seat and having again escaped Pinky's pleas for companionship, the attendant smiled and said, "Would you care for something to drink?"

"Yes please. A red wine."

The attendant placed a little bottle of Mondavi Cabernet Sauvignon on my tray along with a glass. Not a plastic container but a real wine glass. A little perk that I could become accustomed to traveling in a business class seat.

I looked up to thank the attendant for the wine. She was in her twenties with robins egg blue eyes and a winning smile. I had to remember to compliment Pinky concerning his taste in women.

A moment later, I gently leaned back and enjoyed my first taste of a California zinfandel in weeks.

Chapter Thirty-Six

Bear Zabarte—Carson City, Nevada

We'd been back home for a few days and I could tell that Flo wasn't exactly the same as she was before we went to Germany. She was okay during the daytime, but after we went to bed, like an hour later, she'd wake me up with some moaning. The first time I turned on the light, but Flo kept her eyes closed and she kept on moaning. By the third night, I'd had it and moved into Em's empty bed. Hell, Em would't care 'cause she was four hundred miles away at UNLV. In the morning, after I'd get up, I'd make Em's bed so Flo wouldn't know I'd slept there. After the fifth night of Flo's moaning, I called Pinky to see if he knew what I should do.

Some babe answered his phone. "Law office of J. Pinkus Delmont. How may I help you?"

"Babe, first you can tell me who you are, and second why are you answering Pinky's phone instead of that snotty bastard, Robert?"

"Sir, my name is Glinda. I have been sent by Rapid Replacement to answer phones and take messages for Mr. Delmont. I am sorry, but there's no one here named Robert, and I do not know anyone named Pinky."

Jesus, I think I came onto the poor broad like a herd of pissed-off elephants. "Sorry, Glinda. Is the boss there?"

"No sir. There is no one here but me. Would you care to leave a message for Mr. Delmont?"

"Nope. I'll call him at home. Bye."

"Sir, please do not hang up. I would appreciate it if you would leave your name. I've been instructed by Mr. Loomer to record all phone calls to Mr. Delmont."

Damn! All I wanted to do was talk to Pinky about Flo's nightmares, and ask when are we going to get Helmut back from Pacific Grove. Why do I have to go through all this bullshit?

"Okay, write down that Bear called and we need to talk about what he wants me to do about Helmut. Tell Pinky I'll stop by this afternoon."

"Sir, I'm sorry to bother you again, but there still isn't anyone here named Pinky."

That did it. I yelled, "Shit!" into the phone and then slammed it down.

Flo came staggering out of our bedroom. "Why were you screaming at the phone?"

"There's a new broad answering Pinky's phones. First, there was that snarky dude,

Robert, and now there's a clueless broad named Glinda."

She laughed. "Bear, it's good to know that some things don't change. How about we both go to Pinky's office and talk to him after I fix you some corned beef hash for breakfast?"

"Babe, that sounds great, but even that's not gonna make talking to Pinky any easier. The broad answering the bosses phone doesn't even know her boss is named Pinky."

"Then how about we call him at home."

"I was just gonna do that when you walked in." I thought for a second, and then asked, "How was your night? Did you sleep okay?"

Flo looked at me and frowned, "I think so, but even after a full eight hours, I wake up exhausted. Why do you ask?"

Shit, I was afraid she'd ask me that. "Babe, you've been moaning and groaning almost every night since we got back from Germany. It's got so bad that I've been sleeping in Em's bed."

Flo sat down in her chair and a couple of tears started to drip down her cheek. "Bear, I've been having horrible nightmares. No matter how hard I try, the memory of Pinky and I shivering in that cold room, waiting to be killed, won't go away. I'm going to call Willow and ask her if she can recommend a local psychiatrist."

"Babe, I don't think you're ready for the looney bin. Do you really think you need a shrink?"

"I do. Now let's get back to Pinky. Why do you need to talk to him?"

Shit, now I'm between a rock and a hard spot. I was gonna ask Pinky if he was having trouble sleeping, like Flo, but then she'd know that I know she's having trouble sleeping, so I said, "I was wondering when Pinky thinks we should get Helmut back from Pacific Grove."

Flo smiled. "Pacific Grove! I'll bet you ten bucks that a couple of days of walking on the beach and watching the waves come in might help banish my nightmares."

I grabbed my wallet and pulled out a Hamilton. "Babe, you win the bet even before we get to Pacific Grove. I'll call Pinky and—"

The phone rang and I picked it up.

"Mr. Zabarte, this is Glinda. I just talked with Mr. Delmont and he wants to see you, along with a woman named Florence. He told me he'd arrive in fifteen minutes."

"Gotcha." I slammed the phone down. "Babe, get dressed. We've got a meeting with the boss in his office in a few minutes."

My Babe yelled, "Oh my God!" As she ran down the hall she cried, Bear, there is no way in hell that I can shower, dress, and get to that pipsqueak's office in less than an hour. How did he know that I just got up?"

Watching her run down the hall, it seemed to me that life was getting back to normal.

"Babe, take your sweet time. After the last couple of weeks, I'm sure the boss will cut us a little slack."

Chapter Thirty-Seven

Pinky Delmont—Carson City, Nevada

After another troublesome night of Nuremberg nightmares, I arrived at my office around ten to meet a flighty female named Glinda, Loomer's latest attempt to test my tolerance level.

When I walked through the front door, she looked up at me as if I were some sort of aberration. I stopped at her desk and waited for her to introduce herself.

In a quavering voice she said, "Are...you Mr. Delmont?"

"I am. Your name is?"

"Glinda." She stood and held out her hand, as if to shake my hand. "Mr. Delmont, I'm pleased to finally meet you. I have placed on the desk all the messages you have received during your absence. They are in chronological order and—"

"Call Bear. Tell him to be in my office in fifteen minutes, and to bring Florence."

"Yes sir." She hesitated. "Mr. Delmont, a man named Bear left you a message a few minutes ago along with his telephone number.

Could that be the same Bear you just instructed me to call?"

"My dear, just how many men named Bear do you think I know. Yes, you need to call the man named Bear on that message. By the way, please address me as Pinky rather than Mr. Delmont."

"Now I get it. Pinky and Mr. Delmont are the same person."

The office phone rang. "Please excuse me, Mr. Del . . . Pinky. She lifted the receiver and said, "Law Office of J. Pinkus Delmont. Yes, but Mr. Delmont is currently consulting with a client. I will check to see if he can be disturbed."

She hit the hold button and looked to me for further instructions.

"My dear, you handled that call perfectly. Did you get the name of the caller?"

"He said his name was Juri, and he is calling from Nuremberg, Germany."

Excellent!

"I will take his call in my office while you call Bear. If he and Florence arrive while I am still on the phone call with Juri, just send them in."

As I entered my inner sanctum, I considered the possibility that Glinda could become my latest majordomo. She had handled Juri's phone call as a proper gatekeeper. Her knowledge of my office procedures was zero, so her continuing in that position would rely on me convincing Florence to spend a few days training her.

I sat down and picked up the receiver. "Juri, what can I do for you?"

"Pinky, I wanted to let you know that I have canceled the extradition request concerning your client, Helmut Kaufmann, so you can let him out of the place where you have been hiding him."

"Juri, I appreciate your call, but as an officer of the court, I trust you would never think that I would consider hiding a client from a legitimate extradition proceeding."

"Whatever you say, Pinky. By the way, we searched all of the thirty-four concrete buildings and discovered a cache of neo-Nazi paraphernalia in buildings eleven and twelve. Our search turned up recruitment material, a small amount of money, and most importantly, a computer thumb drive that contained the names of one hundred and fifty previously unknown neo-Nazis. And those hundred and fifty names included a dozen police and military officers. I just thought you, Bear and Flo, should know just how much good you accomplished during your brief visit to my city of Nuremberg. Will you please inform them of my government's appreciation for their part in uncovering this important neo-Nazi cell."

"Juri, Bear and Florence are due to meet with me in my office in a few minutes and I will pass on that information. Tell me, did the suicide of Detective Bauman generate a lot of press coverage?"

"Not really. Many in my government feel that press coverage gives the neo-Nazis free advertising. My feeling, however, is the opposite. The more light you can shine on the neo-Nazis, the better. I like to think that had the German people known what Hitler and his henchmen were truly up to, he would never have been able to take over Germany."

"Juri, thank you for your call. I am sorry, but I am in the middle of a meeting with a client."

"And I thought that client ploy was just something you and your secretary had cooked up to screen your calls. Pinky, I look forward to the day when you return to Nuremberg,"

"Thank you, Juri. Goodby,"

I hung up and not sixty seconds later, the intercom buzzed. Glinda said, "Bear and Flo are here to see you."

"Send them in."

The moment the two entered, Bear growled, "Boss, we've got a real problem. Flo's been having crazy nightmares and I've been sleeping in Em's bed 'cause of Flo's moaning. Are you having any trouble sleeping 'cause if you are, we need to know—"

"Bear, cease your babbling!" I commanded. "Florence, is that true?"

Florence nodded, "Yes."

"Then you are in luck. I experienced a similar problem, so I visited Carson City's top psychiatrist. He informed me that I was experiencing PTSD as a result of my Nuremberg experience, and recommended Cognitive Behavioral therapy and medication. The therapy will help me to learn how my memories of the trauma may have impacted my life, and the medication has already helped reduce the nightmares. It should take two to three months of therapy to break the thought cycle that is keeping me trapped in a state of PTSD."

Florence shrugged. "That's interesting Pinky, but I can't afford three months of therapy with Em in college and—"

"My good woman, to assist in the area of personal finance, I have an offer for you. Glinda, the lady sitting at Lu's desk, is the new majordomo for my office. She seems to have the right instincts for the position, but does not know what needs to be done to keep my legal ship on a steady course. It should take no more than a week, perhaps less, of your valuable time. If you agree to help Glinda, I will make you an appointment to see my psychiatrist and pay for all the visits you need to return to your restful pre-PTSD life."

Florence eyed me carefully, as if she could actually see into my soul to determine the validity of my offer.

After a moment of contemplation, she said, "I'll agree to help Glinda, but you'll have to live with your office chaos for a week or so. First, Bear and I are going to rescue Helmut from his isolation in Pacific Grove and take a few days of R and R."

I sat back. Florence and I have sparred many rounds and frankly, at this point, the judges would likely call this bout a draw.

"Florence, I agree to your stipulation. Call Helmut and tell him you will be there soon to return him to Carson City." I waved my hand in the direction of my office door. "You may go."

Bear slammed his giant fist onto my desk. "Damn it, Pinky. We're not a couple of slaves that you can tell, 'you may go', with a wave of your hand."

I could feel a splitting headache coming on. "Of course, my boy. I value you and Florence more than anyone else I know. Now please, leave and bring Helmut back to Carson City."

"Okay," growled Bear. "But we're gonna take a week off. And Flo better have that appointment to see your shrink when she gets back!"

"Florence, as one of the two people in this room who experienced that horrible ordeal, you know you can trust me concerning my psychiatrist."

"I do. Pinky, I'll pick up this conversation next week."

I thought they were about to leave when Bear leaned forward and said, "What about that German dude's book. The one with eight songs. You know, the book you conned out of Helmut?"

"My boy, I did not con the book out of Helmut. He gave it to me as a part of my retainer."

"But did Helmut know that book could be worth a bucket of bucks? Does he know that book was why his uncle was murdered? Does he know that those crazy new-Nazis thought the book was worth so much that once they got their hands on it they could afford to build a pile of atomic bombs?"

My head had started to throb with a rhythmic pulse, not unlike my heartbeat.

"My good man, that book is in my legal possession and as such, whatever happens to the it will be up to me. In fact, when you return from Pacific Grove, I want you to contact Hook to find out the name of his Vegas buyer. This time I will have you, my trusted employee, by my side in case anything untoward should arise. Now, if you two would be so kind, I have work to do."

As Bear and Flo started to leave, Juri's call popped into my head.

"By the way, Juri called and he wanted you to thank you for what you accomplished during your stay in Nuremberg."

Bear said, "Boss, think what a great place the world would be if every cop was like Juri. Okay, we're off to Pacific Grove to get Helmut."

Chapter Thirty-Eight

Bear Zabarte—On the road to Pacific Grove, California

I was cruising along around seventy on Highway 50, just passing Sacramento, when my left tire hit a big hole in the highway pavement. The wheel jumped in my hand and the jolt woke my sleeping Babe up.

She shook her head, fighting for breath like she was coming out of one of those bad dreams.

"Sorry Babe. I tried to miss that chuckhole."

She finally sucked in a big mouthful of oxygen. "That's okay. I needed to wake up."

She stopped talking and stared out the front windshield, like she had forgotten we were on the way to pick up Helmut."

Then, like the real Flo finally woke up, she said, "What's your take on going with Pinky to Vegas so he can cash in that book? What did Hook tell you when you talked with him?"

I glanced at her. Her eyes looked okay and she sounded okay, but some mornings, after a long night of moaning and groaning, she doesn't wake up the same as she used to. Like there was a part of her still stuck inside that cold concrete crapper in Nuremberg.

"Babe, I'll tell you, but first you've got to promise that you won't go all squirrelly on me."

"I can't promise that until you give me your definition of squirrelly."

"Well, I think it means you'll get real nervous. Like you're afraid that Hook might be holding back bad stories about the Vegas mob."

Flo smiled, and said, "Bear, I'm proud of you. That's a pretty good definition. You could add restless, or afraid, but on the whole, you hit the nail on the head. And yes, I'm apprehensive of Hook's observations concerning the Vegas situation."

Shit, now I've got to tell her. "Okay, he told me that there's a guy who wants to buy Pinky's book, but—"

"Somehow I knew there'd be a but," said Flo. "Okay, what's the but?"

"Hook told me that the dude buys all kinds of rare books, and he pays big bucks, but he doesn't play nice with guys who try to stiff him."

"Play nice? What does that mean?"

"If the dude finds out the book is a forgery, then there's a whole lot of empty desert around Vegas that's been used before to hide bodies. Hook's pretty sure that's why Pinky dumped him at the coffee shop and left Vegas on the first plane to Germany. Hook thinks Pinky's scared that his book might be a forgery."

Flo sat back for a second and scrunched her face up, like she was thinking real hard. Then she said, "That sounds like a standard Pinky maneuver. So why does he feel it's safe now to sell the same book to the same guy?"

"Babe, I've been trying to figure that out since we passed Lake Tahoe. My guess is that when those new-Nazi bastards kidnapped you and Pinky, and were gonna do terrible things just to get that stupid book, the boss figured that the book had to be the real McCoy."

"But if the Achtliederbuch turns out to be a forgery, won't you be at risk?"

"I guess so, but we both know I can pretty well take of myself. It's what might happen to the boss that worries me. If cornered, I'm damn sure the little shit would throw me under the bus to save his skin."

Flo sat up. "Then don't go with him to Vegas."

"Babe, somebody's got to keep him alive. Without Pinky, our seat on this gravy train is over. And don't forget that other thing. Pinky's the only reason I didn't spend ten years to life in the slam. So it's like he pays our bills and I still feel like I owe him one."

"Bear, trust me, you've repaid that debt to Pinky ten times over. But if you're going to Vegas with him, you have to promise me that you'll be careful."

"Gotcha, but first we'll join Helmut in Pacific Grove and then we'll spend a couple of days relaxing in a nice quiet place. After that, you can worry what's gonna happen in Vegas."

"Right. I almost forgot about my vacation near the ocean."

The next couple of hours went by with Flo mostly dozing.

Finally, after three hundred miles of dodging cars, pickups, SUVs, and big rigs from Carson City to Pacific Grove, me and Flo unlocked the door at Pinky's condo. I yelled, "Helmut, you can stop hiding. It's just me and Flo. I hope you've still got a couple of cold ones in the fridge."

Chapter Thirty-Nine

Flo Sonderlund—Carson City, Nevada

Generally, the only time I'm asked to provide a chronicle of events is when Bear and I fly, but this time is different. Bear thought I should do this to help out others who might suffer from PTSD but they don't know it. I also gave a copy of this missive to Pinky so he'll know I did get help, but from my female shrink, not his.

Okay, here it goes!

The day before we left Pacific Grove with Helmut, Willow called me.

"Flo, after you told me about your trouble sleeping, I made an appointment for you next Tuesday at 11:00 am with Dr. Ulla Tompkins. In my opinion, she's the top Carson City psychiatrist who specializes in PTSD cases."

I said, "Willow, I think you've jumped the gun here. I'm not sure I even have PTSD. Even if I do, Pinky told me that he would set up an appointment with his guy when I got back to Carson City."

"Flo, we both are well aware of my ex-husband's level of sanity, or lack thereof. Do you really want to discuss your problems with his psychiatrist?"

I chuckled. "Willow, when you put it that way, I can't refuse your kind offer. We'll be home tomorrow and my calendar is clear so anytime she can see me works although I'm still not sure I need to talk with a psychiatrist."

"Flo, over dinner last night Pinky told me all about the kidnapping and imprisonment. Tell me, during that time you two spent in the dark, with hoods over your heads, did you ever feel your life was in danger?"

"Yes, I did, but—"

"No buts. For some reason, civilians like you don't seem to understand that their traumatic experiences require the same treatment as a member of the military or law enforcement. Flo, don't avoid PTSD treatments. I guarantee that once you visit with Dr. Tompkins, you'll quickly realize just how much she can help you."

"Willow, I hear you, but I'm still not convinced that I need help from a shrink."

"Flo, when you go to bed each night, do you sleep through the night or do you have nightmares?"

I had known and respected this woman from the first day I arrived in Carson City. In fact, Willow's only flaw that I could find was that she married Pinky Delmont. But as they are now divorced, she's remedied that single fault.

I said, "Okay, I give up. Thank you for making an appointment for me. I'll let you know what happens."

A few days later, I met Dr. Tompkins and was pleased to discover that she just radiated a positive and pleasant energy.

She didn't ask me to recline on a couch.

She didn't look over her glasses while she took notes.

She didn't even try to convince me that all my problems came from a deep-seated hatred of my mother or father.

She smiled and said, "Find a comfortable chair and please sit down."

I looked around and didn't spot a couch. "Just anywhere?"

"Florence, anywhere you will feel comfortable while we talk."

I sat down in a soft, dark brown leather chair. "Please, call me Flo."

"Good. Flo, generally when the public hears the letters, PTSD they envision a crazed soldier returning from war. Contrary to popular belief, PTSD is not limited to the military. It is a mental health condition that can be triggered by any terrifying event—whether experiencing the event or witnessing the event. All sorts of traumatic occurrences can trigger PTSD, such as a major car accident, an earthquake, or even being kidnapped and threatened with death in Nuremberg Germany."

I nodded. "I see that Willow brought you up to speed concerning my dreadful experience."

"She did. Flo, it is important you understand that PTSD symptoms can include flashbacks, nightmares, along with severe anxiety and a persistent feeling of fear."

"That's interesting to know, Doctor. Presently, my only symptom is the damn nightmares."

She smiled. "Flo, this is very important so listen carefully. Most people who experience traumatic events may temporarily have difficulties adjusting and coping, but with time and good self-care they usually get better. If the symptoms worsen, however, and interfere with your day-to-day functioning, you may need further treatment. Generally, I treat my PTSD patients who require further treatment with psychotherapy. I also prescribe an antidepressant, such as Zoloft or Paxil."

I sat back and considered the three alternatives. I could get better on my own. Then again, I might need psychotherapy, or I could take antidepressants. But before I chose one of the three alternatives, I recalled my dark days before Bear rescued me from my unhappy life in Los Angeles. He lifted me up and gave me the strength I needed to again become the successful woman I had once been.

For that reason, I wasn't one hundred percent sure I could pull myself out of my PTSD without some form of help. But for some reason, psychotherapy was my least preferred choice of the three options offered by the doctor.

That left me with the antidepressant alternative.

"Doctor, it has been less than a month since the kidnapping occurred. Do you think that an antidepressant might help me sleep through the night without those horrible nightmares?"

"I'll have a better handle on that question after you take me through your experience in Nuremberg."

"Really! That's something I've been trying to avoid."

"Avoidance is the worst thing you can do."

So for what felt like an hour, but was probably only twenty minutes, I forced myself to tell the doctor every detail of that time when I was helpless.

"Okay, here it goes. Pinky and I were walking down a street, towards a kiosk, when five men jumped out of a parked van. They gagged us, threw hoods over our heads, tied our hands, pushed us into the van and drove away."

"Slow down, Flo. Take all the time you need to recount each and every detail of your experience."

I did as she asked and as I continued to go over each moment of that horrible time, the mental images became sharper. My hands trembled as I concluded with me huddled next to Pinky, blinded by the hood and waiting to hear that final shot.

I sat back and closed my eyes, to allow that final experience to come into focus. "Doctor, I know this may sound crazy, but I felt like someone who had been dragged in front of a firing squad—hood over my head—and I stood there shaking like a leaf, with an overwhelming fear that each shallow breath I took would be my last."

"Flo, there is one thing we need to agree on during these sessions: there is no such things as a crazy thought. Right?"

I hesitated for a moment, then opened my eyes. "Right."

Doctor Tompkins smiled and said, "Good. Was that the complete experience?"

"Not really. Police Detective Bauman, the Hitler wannabe who threatened to shoot us, turned the gun on himself and blew half his head off.

Doctor Tompkins sat back and brushed a tear from her eye. "Flo, I'd say that experience would trigger frequent nightmares, if not more. For the present, I think a prescription for an antidepressant might solve your sleepless nights. However, before I decide which antidepressant to prescribe, I need a little background on you. Do you have a history of heart disease, high blood pressure, or stroke?"

"No."

"How about liver or kidney disease?"

"No."

"And you are taking warfarin?"

"No."

"Great. Flo, considering what happened to you, I would say that except for your nightmares, you've presented to me a pretty healthy individual. I'm prescribing Zoloft at the lowest initial therapeutic dosage of 25 milligrams for twenty-one days. It is important to take the full course of 21 pills with dinner as follows: The first week take one pill each day. If the nightmares diminish, you can cut down the dosage and take one pill every other day. If after you have taken fourteen pills and your nightmares are gone, take the final seven pills every third day until the bottle is empty. If by that time your nightmares are no more, I will say it has been a pleasure to meet you and I wish you well. However, if the nightmares persist, or return, please call my office and they will set you up for a series of Cognitive therapy sessions."

Feeling much relieved, I stood up and said, "Thank you, Doctor Tompkins. I mean nothing personal, but I truly hope that we never meet again on a professional basis."

The good doctor smiled, "Flo, I agree."

By the time the twenty-one Zoloft pills were gone, my nightmares had vanished.

So there you have it. My brush with PTSD had been resolved with twenty-one magic pills. I fully understand that mine was a mild case of PTSD, but the story does show that there's hope for all of us.

After my nightmares were gone, I called Willow to thank her for all her help.

"Flo, I'm so pleased that you're now peacefully sleeping through the night. Would you mind if I told Pinky about your success with Dr. Tompkins? He still has night tremors."

"Hold on, I thought he went to a psychiatrist before I did?"

Willow sighed, "That's what he told me, but I'm not sure he ever really built enough courage to see a doctor."

I said, "Willow, this is kind of a personal question, but did Pinky have night tremors before he went to Nuremberg?"

"No, they are something new. Flo, no matter what I say, he won't listen to me. Most nights, after he falls asleep he starts shaking and I have to wake him to get him to stop."

I decided that discretion was the better part of valor and didn't ask Willow how she knew of Pinky's night tremors. She's a grown woman. If she feels the need to return to her yo-yo relationship with her ex-husband, so be it. Frankly, I really didn't want to learn any further details.

So with that, Bear, I've done my job and the ball's in your court.

P. S. I trust that Willow will pass on my success story to Pinky. I know he told me that he's seen his psychiatrist, but Pinky's a guy that might lie about that. So I hope that she can convince him to make an appointment to see the person I think is Carson City's top PTSD psychiatrist, Doctor Ulla Tompkins.

Chapter Forty

Pinky Delmont—Carson City, Nevada

After wasting too much of my valuable time working with Glinda, I could not wait any longer for Florence to complete her part of the bargain so I called her.

"Hello."

"Florence, I trust you enjoyed your Pacific Grove respite."

"I did. Pinky, how are your visits going concerning PTSD?"

"My good woman, presently I am too busy to carve out any time. I called you to remind you of our conversation a few weeks ago concerning my office situation. As you recall, Lu's gone, and her replacement Robert left without notice while we were in Nuremberg. Presently, I have a female working in my office named Glinda and—"

"Pinky, I recall your problems with Glinda. Call Loomer and get a replacement."

"The woman seems bright enough but she seems completely unaware that the person sits at that desk does much more than answer phones and take messages."

"Damn it, we both know that your majordomo will never be me. I repeat, call Loomer and get someone who is capable of fulfilling your office requirements."

"Florence, I agreed to cover the cost of your PTSD treatment with my psychiatrist and you agreed to help bring Glinda up to speed—quid pro quo."

"Pinky, I didn't use your psychiatrist and I paid for my own treatment so there isn't any quid pro quo."

"Florence, I have no doubt that spending a few hours each morning training Glinda on the intricacies of running my legal firm will do the job. Could you handle four hours a day for a week?"

"Pinky I'll do as you ask, and as you brought up quid pro quo, it won't cost you an arm and a leg. In exchange for training Glinda four hours a day for one week you will provide me with a two hour professional cleaning service each week for my apartment."

Damn, that woman must have a printed list of demands sitting by her phone, awaiting my next call. "How many months would I be required to provide that exorbitant cleaning service?"

There was a moment of silence, then Florence continued, "For twelve months. That means you will pay for fifty-two, two-hour, cleaning sessions."

I did a quick mental calculation. Based on the cost of my home cleaning service, adjusting down because my home is more than 2500 square feet and her apartment is much smaller, the service should run about $200 per session. So 52 times 200 comes up to $10,400. Thank God, the vixen does not realize that I would spend twice that amount and then some to get my office back to normal.

"Florence, we have a deal. Of course, the final determination concerning the functioning of my office is mine, and mine alone."

"I wouldn't have it any other way. So I can hire a cleaning service and have them send the bills to you, correct?"

'You are correct. And I will expect to see you in my office tomorrow morning."

"I'll be there tomorrow morning at 8:30 sharp for my first of five days. Right now I'm going to put my vacuum cleaner away hopefully for the last time, sit down and watch a Jeopardy rerun."

"Thank you, Florence. One more item, one of the tasks I require from my majordomo is to be sure my credenza is fully stocked with my favorite single malt Scotch whiskey. Please remember to point out that vitally important item to Glinda."

"I'll even take Glinda to your favorite liquor store after lunch. Then she'll know where to buy your expensive booze the next time."

"Excellent."

"Bye now."

That almost seemed easy. I set my phone down and was about to go over my closing arguments on a minor court case, when I heard a tentative knock on my office door.

"Yes?"

Glinda said, "You have a client waiting by my desk and he needs to talk with you."

I guessed that it was likely Helmut Kaufmann, who felt the need to stop by and show his appreciation for my latest legal magic act. I said, "Fine, send him in."

She left and closed the door to my office. A moment later the door burst open and there stood Hook making circles with that damned stainless-steel tip over his head.

I jumped up and forced a smile, an action that I hoped would paper over my near crippling apprehension. "My good man, what a pleasant surprise."

My mind raced for a way to tell Glinda to call the police. "Please sit down, Hook."

Once he sat down, I glanced at my desk calendar, intercom, anything to distract my attention off that hook.

I said "Pardon me Hook, but I need to check my calendar with Glinda, that lovely young lady you passed. The poor thing is so new that she has trouble navigating the court computer system. If you will excuse me for a moment, I will make sure we are not interrupted for a scheduled court date."

I jumped up and shot out of my office before Hook could respond, much less move to block my exit. After I escorted Glinda back to her desk, I leaned over and whispered, "Call the police at once. Both of our lives depend on you making that call."

I turned and before I entered my office, I forced a casual swagger as I walked to my desk. "My schedule is clear for the next hour. Now, Hook, what can I do for you?"

He held the sharp point of his hook above my newly repaired desk, no more than a quarter of an inch from the last gouge that the steel point dug a few weeks earlier.

I stared at Hook's expression, and was wary that for some reason, he seemed calm.

"Pinky, before I came here, I got a call from Bear."

My heart skipped a beat as I listened for the sound of a siren, any sign of my pending rescue by a cadre of Carson City's finest.

"And?"

"Bear informed me that you and him are planning on making a trip to Vegas. You'll still need my help to set up some kind of a meeting between you and the man who buys old books."

"You are correct, Hook. I was about to call you and explain, but—"

"Shyster, don't bullshit me. I know that you want to sell that book, but me and you already drove to Vegas where you skipped out and left me sitting in a Denny's with nothing but a cup of coffee."

"I recall that day as clearly as if it happened an hour ago. While I was in the Denny's bathroom, I received a call from Florence, you recall, Bear's lady friend. She told me that she and Bear were in trouble and they required my immediate assistance in Nuremberg. My good man, Nuremberg is in Germany! That meant I had to leave on the next flight from McCarran Field International to Germany. I called Robert to let you know of the abrupt change in my plan and told him to give you a check for $15,000 for your trouble."

"Shyster, that first check was okay, but I'm not gonna give you the name of the man in Vegas without fifteen more big ones."

For a few seconds we stared at each other. We both knew that I was not obliged to give him a second check for $15,000. But I also understood that a second check would buy me out of what had become an untenable situation.

"Hook, I believe that $10,000, considering your lack of involvement in this second trip, would be a more appropriate amount.

I held my breath during his moment of consideration. Then he nodded and pulled his hook away from my desk.

I grabbed my phone, hit the intercom button, and said, "Glinda, please cut a check for ten thousand dollars payable to Mr. Dudek."

I set my phone down. "Hook, now that we have reached common ground, I trust you will provide Bear with the name and address of the gentleman in Vegas."

I glanced at my calendar. "Now, if you will excuse me, I have a court appearance in less than an hour."

Hook glared at me and then he jumped up. "I'll give Bear the name and address once the check clears."

Once that stainless weapon had exited my office I jumped up and locked the door to my inner sanctum.

I allowed Hook a good ten minutes to receive his extortion check and leave my building. Then I quietly unlocked and opened my office door. Glinda was the only person in the room, so I casually walked toward her desk.

"Glinda, I gave you specific instructions to call the police. What happened?"

"Two officers arrived inside of five minutes, but as I had not been given the reason why you needed them, they left."

My first impulse was to scream at her, but then I realized my last instructions concerning Hook Dudek had been delivered to Robert, not to the lovely young lady sitting before me.

Controlling my anger, I realized that did not know much about Glinda beyond what she was not.

She was not a replacement for the stoic, phlegmatic Lu.

She was not a loud, brash paraplegic named Robert V Silva.

In fact, the woman struck me as an energetic person who wanted to please her employer. I pondered my latest situation. After the revolving door of secretarial employees, Loomer's statement about my reputation as a difficult boss made me consider there might be a modicum of truth in his admonition.

"Glinda, in the future, if Mr. Dudek enters the building you are to call the police and inform them that Mr. Dudek has threatened my life."

"Pinky, is that true?"

"Of course it is."

"Right. In the future I will call the police. Tell me, is he a disgruntled client?"

"No, just a very angry man. Glinda, I almost forgot. Tomorrow morning a woman named Florence will help you learn the intricacies of your new position as my new majordomo. Once she decides you understand the demands of your new title, you will receive a ten percent increase in your salary."

"Majordomo? A ten percent raise? I'm thrilled, but Pinky, I don't have a clue what a majordomo is or does."

"Florence will explain all that to you beginning tomorrow morning. Don't worry Glinda, you are about to embark on an epic journey and I am positive we will get along splendidly."

Chapter Forty-One

Bear Zabarte—Carson City, Nevada

Me and Flo were watching TV when Pinky called and told me he was gonna drive to Vegas to meet the dude who's gonna buy his book. Then he told me I had to go with him. I told him that I was in the middle of a hot game of Cribbage with Flo and I'd call him back as soon as the game was over.

It's funny how weird things pop into your head when you need to stall for time when talking to Pinky. For some strange reason, when he told me I had to go with him to Vegas, playing Cribbage with my Grandpa Zabarte popped into my head. Shit, Grandpa taught me how to play Cribbage like my life depended on winning. The year I met Flo, I tried to play Cribbage with her but after I skunked her a couple of times she never wanted to play with me again.

So now you know that I wasn't really playing Cribbage with Flo when Pinky called.

Flo said, "Why did you tell him that? I hate that stupid game. We're sitting here watching Jeopardy."

"I know that, but I wanted to talk to Hook before I gave Pinky my answer."

"Bear, we're an investigative team. That means I'm just as important a cog in this wheel as you are. What was Pinky's question?"

What does a wheel have to do with anything? "Babe, he wants me to go to Vegas with him."

"To sell that book? Before we flew to Germany I told Pinky that it was unethical for him to sell a forgery to an uninformed buyer."

"Babe, I don't know anything about—"

"You tell Pinky that you and I are a team and this team member won't be a part of his nefarious scheme."

I'd lived with Flo long enough to know that Pinky hadn't asked her, he'd asked me, but this was one of those times to shut my pie hole and leave it at that.

"Babe, I'll go in the bedroom to call Hook, so you can watch Jeopardy in peace."

I tiptoed away to the bedroom, dialed Hook's number, and asked him what he thought about me going to Vegas with Pinky to sell his book.

"Bear, don't trust him. If it hadn't been for my girlfriend, I'd still be sitting at that booth in Denny's. One word of advice, the Vegas dude I was setting him up with is connected. That means Pinky's book had better be legit or the shit is gonna hit the fan."

Jesus, I didn't know Hook had a girlfriend. I wonder if she keeps one eye on that hook when there're foolin' around. "Hook, I'll be okay 'cause Pinky knows better then to leave me sitting in a booth at Denny's."

"How do you know that for sure?"

"'Cause he knows I'd smack him so hard that he'd need a wheelchair to get around, like Robert, that snarky dude who took over for Lu."

"I remember him. You're right. He was a snarky dude."

"Not anymore. Pinky's got a new babe named Glinda."

Hook said, "Yah. I met her yesterday when I was in Pinky's office. Bear, wasn't Glinda the name of the good witch in the Wizard of Oz?"

"Got me. You'd have to ask Flo that. Thanks for the stuff on Pinky and Vegas."

"Bear, I'm pretty sure her name was Glinda. I used to read *The Wizard of Oz* to the third-grade classes at Carson Elementary. By the way, I just emailed you the name and address of the man in Vegas that Pinky wants to meet."

"Thanks. See you around. Bye."

I hung up fast before Hook had the chance to say any more.

323

Then I called Willow, explained that me and Pinky were going to Vegas to sell his book and asked her what she thought.

She said, "Bear you'd be crazy to walk into the lion's den."

I said, "Willow you're confused. we're going to Vegas, not to a zoo to see some lions.

She sighed and said, "Heaven help you both."

I never did figure out what driving to Vegas to see lions had anything to do with Pinky selling his book.

So, after a bunch of worthless advice from Flo, Hook, and Willow, I called Pinky and told him I'd go with him to Vegas. Why? 'Cause I was afraid one of those Mafia goombas might dump him into a hole and throw dirt on him. Then me and Flo would have to look for a new job.

Anyway, Pinky told me he'd pick me up after two am I asked him why we were driving to Vegas at that ungodly hour. He told me he wanted to get to Vegas around ten in the morning.

He picked me up about 2:15 and I climbed into his new Mercedes for the first time,. Shit, I had to admit that his car was one cool bucket of bolts.

Pinky said, "I took a four-hour nap and I am as fresh as a daisy, so all you have to do is sit back and enjoy the scenery."

"Boss, it's darker out there then the insides of a black dog. How about I drive for a couple of hours?"

"Let you take the wheel of my new car? Not on your life. As I said, just sit back and relax."

One of the funny things about riding in an electric car is there's not a lot of noise. In fact, there's no noise. So after about fifteen minutes of trying to find something interesting to look at in the dark, I fell asleep. The next thing I knew was Pinky shaking me.

"Bear, we are on the outskirts of downtown Tonopah. Although I do not need to charge up my Mercedes, I will do so while we recharge our human batteries with a hot breakfast."

Still a little dopey from sleeping, I followed Pinky into a warm restaurant.

Pinky ordered something called the Silver Miner's special while I ordered three scrambled eggs with two giant biscuits smothered with what the menu claimed was the best white sausage gravy in Nevada, if not the whole world. The weird thing is the menu was almost right. I don't know if that gravy was the best in the whole world, but it was the best I'd ever eaten.

I was wiping up a puddle of that great gravy with a piece of biscuit when I heard a loud bang outside the restaurant. I glanced out the big window just in time to see the back end of Pinky's Mercedes start to smoke.

I jumped up and yelled, "Boss, there's smoke pouring out of the trunk of your new car."

Pinky took one look, and cried, "Oh my God, that is my car!"

He jumped up and ran out of the restaurant with me right behind him.

By the time we reached the car, the back end was a full-blown bonfire, and burning hotter than hell.

Pinky started to run toward the trunk. I grabbed him and pulled him back so the little twerp wouldn't end up a crispy critter.

"Boss, you go any closer and you'll look like a chicken fried steak."

He kept trying to pull away from me. "Let me go, you oaf. My priceless first edition is inside that trunk."

"Boss, stop and take a good look. The trunk of the car has burned and now the front is going up too. Your book is ashes by now."

We both stood there, so close to the flames that the heat was curling the hair on my arm. Finally, even Pinky could see that his fancy new car was a goner, a burned out hulk, and he stopped trying to pull away.

That was about when I heard the sirens of a local fire truck. About a minute later the truck pulled up. Fire fighters and a whole bunch of people from the restaurant stood with me and Pinky, cooked on the frontside while our backsides shivered in the cold early morning. We watched until Pinky's brand-new Mercedes turned into a stinky, burned out, twisted pile of metal, plastic, and rubber.

The fire dude with the biggest hat turned to Pinky and said, "Buddy, excuse me, but was that your car?"

Pinky, looking sorta like he'd just been hit upside the head with a 2x4, gave him a little nod.

The fire dude continued, "This is the second one of these EV fires we've had in Tonopah this year. I know those new electric cars are great, but all of them have got one little design flaw, lithium-ion batteries. Once those babies catch fire it's all over." He shook his head. "Sorry, buddy, but those cars burn so hot that once they get going, even us trained firefighters can't put them out. About all we can do is let the car burn, and keep the public as far back as possible.

Like his brain finally figured out that his life-time meal ticket was gone forever, Pinky turned and looked at me. It might have been ash or something else, but I'll swear on a stack of Bibles that an actual tear slipped out of Pinky's eye and trickled down his cheek.

"Bear, you had better call Florence. I fear we are in need of a rescue."

Chapter Forty-Two

Flo Sonderlund—Carson City, Nevada

I'd gone to bed a little after ten, still upset that Bear decided to accompany Pinky to Vegas. And then I woke up when Pinky picked up Bear. The clock radio showed it was 2:15.

I rolled over and spent the next thirty minutes tossing and turning in a futile attempt to clear the apprehensions from my mind.

Eventually I drifted off, then almost jumped out of my skin when my phone rang. It took me a second to focus my eyes and read that the time was 5:45.

"Hello?"

"Babe, it's me. We were eating breakfast in Tonopah when Pinky's new car caught fire and burnt up. I know it's early, but can you grab the truck and come get us?"

My mind was starting to comprehend what Bear just told me. I said, "Bear, are you and Pinky okay?"

"Yup."

"Did Pinky's Achtliederbuch burn with the car?"

"Yup."

"Okay, I'm getting up. I'll leave as soon as I get dressed and see you in a few hours in Tonopah."

"Babe, before you go, Pinky wants to ask you something. I'll hand him my phone."

"Florence, thank you for rescuing us. Now, before you start your drive, I have a simple question that I would like you to ponder while you wend your way through the dark desert to Tonopah. Why were you a hundred percent positive that my Achtliederbuch was a fake?"

Pinky's question stopped me for a second. "Because everyone I queried told me it was nearly impossible that the book was genuine."

"Not everyone, Florence. The neo-Nazis thought the Achtliederbuch was worth strangling Helmut's uncle. And then they kidnapped us and were ready to kill us for the book. And Detective Bauman blew his brains out because he was not going to take possession of the Achtliederbuch. Is it possible that they knew something concerning that book you did not know?"

I sat on the edge of the bed Bear and I share, my feet dangling an inch above the carpet. At that moment, I had the sinking feeling that in this world almost anything was possible, even the million to one chance that Pinky's Achtliederbuch was the real thing.

"Pinky, I don't have a clue if the neo-Nazis knew more than I did. And considering the condition of the book that resides in your burnt up car, any questions concerning the authenticity of the Achtliederbuch is long past the point of debate.

"See you and Bear in a few hours. Bye now!"

Three hours later, as I drove through the desert in the pastel light of daybreak, I thanked my lucky stars that the Achtliederbuch was out of our lives. That book had caused nothing but trouble the moment it landed in Pinky's hands. However, if I'm completely honest, the knowledge that Pinky missed out on a massive payout kept a smile on my face all the way to the city limits of Tonopah.

Author's Notes

The inspiration for *The Heretics Hymnal* was handed to me during a visit to Wittenberg, Germany, the town where Martin Luther lived and died.

While taking a tour of Martin Luther's home, now a museum, a docent held up a book and stated, "The item I hold in my hand is a second edition of Martin Luther's famous eight song book, or the Achtliederbuch in German.

Before she could move on to present the next object, I raised my hand and asked, "Why does the museum have a second edition rather than a first edition?"

She blinked, as if no one had ever asked that question before. "Because a first edition of the Achtliederbuch has never been found."

I asked, "If someone did discover a first edition, what would be its value?"

She thought for a moment and then said, "Priceless!"

Bingo!

The docents 'priceless' valuation created the MacGuffin for this mystery.

What's a MacGuffin? It's a term for an object or element in a story that drives the plot. It usually takes the form of a mysterious artifact that everyone in the story is chasing. In this case, the Achtliederbuch is *The Heretics Hymnal's* MacGuffin.

So the Achtliederbuch provided the plot, but at the time I was working a different book. It took me another year, while visiting Nuremberg, Germany, before the plot came together while touring the unfinished Congress Hall and later, Zeppelin Field.

First the Congress Hall. The exterior of Congress Hall is pictured below.

It looks like a big, solid building on the outside.

A few minutes later we took a right turn and entered what should have been the inside of a building. The amazing part is there wasn't a building at all, just a three or four story high wall of reddish brick.

What happened to the building?

That answer is easy. The interior of the building was never built. Only the exterior wall. Why? Because Hitler was spending all of Germany's money on war.

Here is a picture of the inside of Congress Hall.

The inside of Congress Hall is what the Texan's would call all hat and no cattle.

And now to Zeppelin Field.

The picture below shows how a Zeppelin Field rally looked in 1936, followed by how Zeppelin Field looks today.

Zeppelin Field—1936

Zeppelin Field—Today

The last photo shows five of the thirty-four concrete buildings where Pinky and Flo were taken to be disposed of as soon as the kidnappers got their hands on the Achtliederbuch.

These 34 buildings were constructed in a big arc opposite the grandstands. Built as toilet facilities to be used during the massive rallies. Bear called them 'concrete crappers'.

If you have any comments or questions, please feel free to email me at ken@kendalton.com